Trickery of the Witch

Crypt Witch cozy paranormal mystery series - book 7

K.E. O'Connor

K.E. O'Connor Books

While every precaution has been taken in the preparation of this book, the publisher assumes no responsibility for errors or omissions, or for damages resulting from the use of the information contained herein.

All rights reserved.

No portion of this book may be reproduced in any form without written permission from the publisher or author, except as permitted by U.S. copyright law.

TRICKERY OF THE WITCH

Copyright © 2022 by K.E. O'Connor

ISBN: 978-1-915378-05-7

Written by: K.E. O'Connor

Chapter 1

"Move over a bit, Tempest. I've got no room." My cousin, Azura nudged me with her elbow.

I shifted over, but there was barely any space around the crowded table in Mom's kitchen. Everyone was there, including my cousins, Azura and Raine, who'd arranged a last-minute visit and were staying for the weekend.

"Ouch! You're squashing my foot." Aurora sat on my other side, smooshed between Uncle Kenny and me.

"It's not my fault we don't have a bigger table." I grabbed for the bread as it passed by, taking two white slices so I wouldn't be left with the healthy wholemeal.

"It's great to have you all here." Auntie Queenie bustled in and kissed Raine and Azura's cheeks in turn. "My girls so rarely visit. This is a perfect surprise." She shoved her way into a seat next to Uncle Kenny and helped herself to a mountain of creamed potato.

"It was Raine's idea," Azura said, a mirror of her sister with pale skin and black hair. "She announced a couple of days ago that we were coming to Willow Tree Falls."

Raine shrugged. "What can I say? I missed you all."

"Of course you did, darling," Auntie Queenie said.

"We're always happy to have you." Mom hurried around the table, checking that everyone had enough to eat.

"You'll have to come to Cloven Hoof one night," I said.

"Definitely," Azura said. "I love it there. Have you got those mushrooms that make you feel all floaty and giggly?"

"Always."

Raine nodded, her mouth full of food. "We'll be there."

Wiggles' paws settled on my knees, and he pressed down hard to get my attention.

I peered at him. "What are you doing?"

"Avoiding being crushed to death by so many feet. Get me out of here. I've already had my tail trodden on twice."

I shoved my seat back and pulled him onto my lap.

He grabbed a potato from my plate and swallowed it whole.

"If you do that again, I'm putting you back under the table to face trial by sweaty feet."

"It's the only way I can get food," he said. "It's like a pack of vultures around this table."

"It's grab it and growl around here when we're all together," Granny Dottie said with a chuckle. She tossed Wiggles a piece of bread, which he caught in mid-air.

It was rare my entire family got together. Someone always needed to keep an eye on the demon prison. Not today. We had spells in place to alert us of any trouble, and the demons were on their best behavior ever since the extra protection spells were put in place. It was a precautionary measure following a near miss when the demons revolted and tried to escape.

The new spells stung them like a mass of angry hornets and helped to remind them that no one broke out of a prison guarded by the Crypt witches.

I looked around the crowded table and smiled. When the family converged in one place, it was always like this. Everyone talked over each other, excited to share their news and find out what everyone else was doing.

It felt good to be surrounded by this kind of chaos. It had been a tricky couple of months since we'd almost lost Aurora to her unscrupulous fiancé, but finally, things were getting back to normal.

I nudged Aurora with my elbow. "How's the food?"

She pushed her potato salad around with a fork. "Good."

"Did you see the apple pie Mom made?"

"I think I'll skip dessert," she said.

My eyebrows rose. Aurora never skipped dessert. She'd been down ever since discovering her fiancé was a lying, deceitful swine. Her usually bubbly personality had been squashed by him, and she was struggling to get back to her old self. I worried she might never get over what Toby did to her.

"You know what you need." I leaned closer to Aurora, even though only inches separated us. "To go out on a few dates. Find somebody to make you laugh again."

She shook her head, her gaze downcast. "Not a chance."

"You're not interested in getting a new boyfriend?"

"Absolutely not. What's the point? You can't trust any of them."

That definitely wasn't Aurora talking. She was usually the cheery one. I could be, well, a little grumpy at times. We balanced each other out.

"Some of them aren't so bad. Rhett's decent," I said.

"Rhett's also a fallen angel, who heads up a biker gang," Aurora said. "Hardly a glowing character reference."

I didn't miss the sharpness in her tone. I let it slide. She was having a rough time. "I'm not saying you need to find someone to marry, but someone who'll show you a good time wouldn't be a bad thing."

"You don't want to stay out of the saddle too long," Granny Dottie said way too loudly, obviously listening in to the conversation. "You don't want your skills to get rusty."

I shook my head at Granny Dottie. Now wasn't the time for her to dish out her pearls of wisdom when it came to romance.

She continued, ignoring my signal to put a sock in it. "How about that charming Tate from Mystic Mushroom? I'm always trying to get him married off."

Aurora lowered her fork. "Tate's nice. I'm just not interested in a relationship. I've decided to stick to work and not think about love. I intend to expand Heaven's Door. I let things slide when I was with Toby, and I've lost customers."

"They'll be back," I said. "No one can resist your store for long." Heaven's Door always smelled of brownies, vanilla, and hope. Aurora always had a smile and a solution for every customer.

She sighed. "I hope so. Still, that will be my focus for now. Maybe forever."

Wiggles rested his head on her knees, his back end splayed across my thighs. "I'll be your furry boyfriend if you ask nicely."

She petted his head. "That's sweet of you. Where shall we go on our first date?"

He flipped on his back and exposed his belly. "Give me a rub while I think about it. Do you like muddy holes and sticks?"

Aurora obliged with a belly rub. "Not so much."

"Then we might have a problem," Wiggles said.

"How about you get a pet, like Wiggles?" I said.

Aurora lifted her gaze to mine. A little sparkle of happiness appeared in her blue eyes. "That's not a bad idea. I don't have a familiar."

My mouth twisted to the side. "I hadn't thought about you getting a familiar, but why not?" Familiars were magic users' companions. They healed and enhanced magic and came in all different forms, from cute dogs to enormous owls.

Wiggles was definitely not a familiar and marched firmly to the beat of his own stubby paws while stealing food and talking back. But he was my best buddy, and although he could be a huge pain in my behind, I wouldn't change him.

"That's a great idea," Mom said. "A familiar will be excellent company, Aurora. They can help you in the store while you get everything back together."

"Cats. That's what you should stick to," Auntie Queenie said. "You never see our three giving you problems."

I arched a brow. That was debatable. Mom, Granny Dottie, and Auntie Queenie had three black cats as their familiars. They were spiky, difficult, and rude to everybody apart from them.

"Let's finish here and go to Fur Baby Emporium," I said. "Abigail always has plenty of familiars for sale."

Wiggles grunted. "Do I have to come? Abigail might try to sell me because of my unique skill set."

"Your skill set is stealing from the trash and breaking wind," I said. "Who would find that desirable?"

"You do."

I rubbed his head. I sort of did.

"You absolutely must come with us," Aurora said. "You can give me advice on suitable familiars."

"So long as there are doughnuts involved afterwards, I'm in," he said.

Aurora touched my arm, and she smiled. "Thanks, Tempest. It's a great idea. I would like some company. I get lonely on my own now that, well, now things are different."

I grimaced. I was glad she didn't say Toby's name in front of everyone. It always riled people up when they were reminded of what happened.

She'd been living with Toby before his lies had been exposed, and it would take her a while to get used to her own company again. But if she got a familiar, she'd have nothing to worry about. Problem solved.

We raced through the rest of lunch, and I grabbed three slices of apple pie to go from Mom before hurrying out the front door.

As much as I loved my family, they were chaotic and noisy. I was more into the chilled, relaxed vibe at my club, Cloven Hoof. Short periods of exposure to my family I could handle. Anything else and I got stressed and started to snap.

We walked side-by-side, taking bites of our pie as Wiggles romped ahead. It had been a stressful few months. I'd come so close to losing my sister. My blood chilled every time I thought about how we almost lost her.

The same went for Frank, my incumbent demon. I'd had a blissful few days when he hadn't been living inside me, but he was also back, and amazingly, he was on his best behavior. He'd also had a shock at the thought of never being able to get his demon claws into my sister. For now, he seemed content to be in her presence. It wouldn't last; it never did.

Right now, everything was good. I had my sister back, her sleazy ex-fiancé was never getting out of prison, and Willow Tree Falls basked in a fabulous spell of sunshine.

Plus, everything was good at Cloven Hoof. The clientele was rarely a problem, the staff were happy, and my relationship with Rhett was great. My life had never felt so stable.

"Hey, look! It's Axel," Aurora said. "And isn't that one of his sisters?"

I nodded as Axel Shadowsoul strolled toward us.

He lifted a hand. "The Crypt sisters. Great to see you. You know my sister, Foxglove." He gestured to the darkly gorgeous woman next to him dressed in a fitted black cat suit and a leather jacket.

"Sure. Nice to see you again," I said.

She nodded. "I'm checking up on my brother and making sure he's not getting in too much trouble." Foxglove had a melodious tone to her voice. Just like Axel, she was a half-demon.

"Axel has his moments," I said. "Although, recently, he's been behaving himself."

"Keep quiet about that," he said. "I have a reputation to keep intact."

"It's Merrie's good influence," I said. Axel had been dating my bar manager, Merrie Noble, for months. It was the longest relationship he'd been in, and she was certainly doing him good. Although he still came with a dark edge, it was tinged with happiness. Being in a stable relationship suited Axel.

"Oh, yes. We're going to meet her later," Foxglove said. "I'm looking forward to meeting the woman who's finally tamed my brother."

He shrugged, and his cheeks flushed. "I'm not tamed."

"You shouldn't protest. Being tamed suits you," I said. "So long as you're treating Merrie right, I fully endorse the relationship."

Axel tugged at the neck of his shirt. "Everyone's making out like it's such a big deal. I have dated women before."

His pink cheeks and shifty glances showed he also thought it was a big deal. I grinned at him. "Introducing Merrie to one of your sisters must mean things are serious."

"Tempest, quit it," he muttered.

Aurora's smile faded. "It's nice to see someone's relationship is working."

I tucked my hand through her elbow, sensing a dip in her fragile happiness. "We need to get on. Nice to see you, Foxglove."

She nodded. "You too. I'll drop by the club one evening, and we can catch up. You can tell me all about Axel's sickeningly good behavior."

"It's a date. See you there." I walked away with Wiggles and Aurora.

She sighed and dragged her feet.

"Hey, things will get better. It's only been a couple of months since the whole Toby incident," I said.

"We're not saying his name, remember," she said. "Every time I think about him, I want to die of shame."

"I'm not denying that you have lousy taste in guys," I said. "But now that you know what you definitely don't want, you can focus on what you do."

"I don't want a boyfriend," Aurora said. "I'm sticking to work. And maybe a familiar, as long as we find the right one."

"Then focus on that. Let's go have some fur-filled fun and find you a true love who won't turn you into a stone dragon."

Chapter 2

Stepping into Fur Baby Emporium was like walking into a magical zoo. The air was alive with the chatter of animals, from chirping canaries with multi-colored feathers to giant tortoises that munched on enormous hunks of lettuce.

Abigail Furby had run the emporium for more than a decade. She loved her animals and had a natural way with any magical creature, whether it had fur, feathers, or scales.

The door closed behind us gently, and I took a moment to take in the animals all around us. There were shelves of large, well-maintained cages, and a number of magical familiars were free-roaming, including several owls sitting on high perches and numerous cats.

"Wow! Take a look at that snake." Aurora dropped my arm and headed toward a large glass-fronted enclosure. A huge python with glistening green scales stared back at her, its tongue flickering in and out, tasting the air.

"That's Goliath." Abigail appeared along the aisle and hurried toward us. A cloud of dark brown curls floated around her head, and she wore a flowered dress over her generous curves.

"Hi, Abigail," Aurora said. "I'm in need of your expert help."

Her big dark eyes widened as she clapped her hands together. "You're looking for a familiar. I can sense it about you. There comes a time in every witch's life when she needs a constant companion. And, given your recent... difficulties, this is just the thing you need."

Aurora glanced at me and swallowed. "I agree. It's time I had someone to rely on."

"And you're thinking a snake?" Abigail tilted her head. "They're a very particular kind of magical familiar. And Goliath is one-of-a-kind. I've had him ever since I opened the store. I'm rather fond of him."

"Definitely not a snake," Aurora said. "He's beautiful, and I was just admiring his gleaming scales, but I need something smaller."

"I can show you cats, dogs, rabbits, plenty of different birds. How about an owl? A wise, sensible familiar. That could be just what you need."

I leaned toward Aurora and lowered my voice. "Is she suggesting you're not wise?"

Aurora glared at me. She turned her attention back to Abigail. "Yes, let's start with an owl. They're so beautiful. Not a large one, though."

"How about a Small Owl? They live up to their name," Abigail said. "Good-natured, reliable, and you can almost fit one in your purse. They're excellent at enhancing spells relating to healing. You must sell a lot of those in your store."

"I like the sound of that." Aurora nodded. "Show me what you've got."

I stayed back with Wiggles as Abigail and Aurora studied several cute mini owls. I glanced down at him. "Do we have room in our lives for a familiar?"

"Nope. I'm more than enough for you," Wiggles said. "You don't need a familiar when you have a hellhound who breathes fire."

"You don't enhance my magic, though." That was the great thing about familiars. Not only were they natural protectors of whoever they chose to live with, and make no mistake, familiars chose you, not the other way around, but their magic melded with yours. It was like giving your ability a triple espresso shot with a side order of wowsers. Familiars were awesome.

"Your apartment's too small for a familiar," Wiggles said. "Besides, we've got everything set up just as we like it. You have your bedroom, and I have everywhere else."

"You sleep on my bed," I said.

"I sometimes use my bed in the lounge," he said. "You've got enough going on looking after me. Adding a familiar will only make things harder for you. I'm just thinking of you. Always you."

"Thanks for worrying about me," I said with a smirk. "You really don't think we have room for one of these cute little kittens?" I slid a finger into a cage where three bright blue-eyed kittens stared back at me and mewed appealingly.

Wiggles pulled himself up on his front paws and stared in the cage. "We're not getting a cat. They smell funny."

One of the kittens swiped at his nose, and he reared back.

"This one could be my perfect familiar." I tickled a kitten under its tiny chin. "You could play together. Don't you get lonely?"

"I have you," Wiggles said. "And you don't come with claws."

"Sometimes, I have to work. And I don't take you on my dates with Rhett."

"Which I'm not happy about," Wiggles said. "What do you do on these dates that I can't see?"

I snorted a laugh. "Discuss the latest books we've read."

Smoke drifted from his mouth. "A likely story. Besides, when you work, I hang out in the bar and keep the guests entertained. A familiar wouldn't do that. These kittens look boring."

The kittens glared at Wiggles and hissed, their tiny tails puffing out comically.

I grinned as I retracted my finger. "Maybe not a kitten. They've already got the measure of you."

He snorted at the kittens before dropping to the ground. "Let's leave the familiars to Aurora."

Aurora stood with a mini owl balanced on her outstretched arm. She was listening intently to Abigail as she talked to her about the owl.

"I hope this helps. She's been different since being messed around by Toby."

"No kidding," Wiggles said. "He lied to her, turned her into some Stepford wife witch, and then when she figured out what he was up to, he transformed her into a stone dragon and left her outside his front door. That's going to leave a mark."

"Aurora's always been the easy-going one," I said. "I don't suit easy-going and smiley. My face hurts when I smile too much."

"Frowning too much gives you wrinkles."

"Thanks for that," I said. "I mainly frown because you misbehave."

"I bring joy to your life," he said. "Some smelly familiar would never do that."

A growl had me turning on my heel and ducking to find the source of the noise. Tucked underneath the cages was a grubby ginger cat.

Wiggles took a step back. "That has got to be the ugliest cat I've ever seen. Is Abigail trying to sell that thing?"

I peered at the cat. It didn't look in great condition. She was a bit thin and definitely needed a bath. I held out my hand, but the cat hissed and backed up a step.

"Maybe the cat belongs to Abigail," I said.

"If so, she's not doing a great job of looking after her." Wiggles lifted his nose. "She also stinks. And not like a usually hot, furry cat smell."

The cat growled again.

"She also doesn't like you," I said. "Leave her alone and stop telling her she smells funny."

"It's a dumb cat. She doesn't understand me," Wiggles said.

I tilted my head. There was something different about this cat. This wasn't your average ginger kitty. She had a vibe of magic about her.

Wiggles lowered on to his belly. "I'll get her out."

"You really shouldn't," I said. "She's given you a warning."

"I'm not afraid of her." He wriggled closer.

The cat growled menacingly.

"What have you got under there?" Abigail hurried over.

"Is this cat yours?" I asked.

She peered under the cages. "Oh! No, definitely not. She turned up a few weeks ago. She must have snuck in the door when someone walked in. I can't seem to get rid of her."

"Maybe she's looking for a home," I said.

"Not here," Abigail said. "She's bad tempered. Come on. Out you get." She waved a hand at the door.

"I'll deal with her. I can almost touch her." Wiggles shuffled closer. "Eek!" He shot backwards. "She scratched me!"

"I warned you. Have you got some food to get her out?" I asked Abigail. "She needs a good meal. That might cheer her up."

"I don't like to encourage her." Abigail sighed. "Still, I need her out of the store. It won't look good for business if there's some poor mangy old ginger cat stuck under a cage. Like you did, customers will think I have something to do with her rather sad condition."

The cat hissed at her as if she understood what Abigail was saying.

"Are you sure she's not a familiar?" I asked.

"Absolutely! I can always sense familiars. I'll be back in a moment." Abigail strode away.

"Get out of there, you manky furball," Wiggles said, keeping well out of the swiping range of the cat as he licked at his scratched nose.

"Stop annoying her," I said.

"You heard Abigail. That cat has to go." He ducked and glared at the cat. "I bet she's got fleas."

"Wiggles, maybe you—"

The cat shot out from under the cage as if propelled on a rocket. She jumped on Wiggles' back and dug her claws in before snapping her teeth at his ear.

Wiggles howled and rolled over, sending the cat flying. He jumped to his feet and hopped around, trying to find her. "Did you see that? Did you see what she did? I'll catch rabies."

I bit my bottom lip and tried not to laugh at the indignant look on his face. He had one hundred percent asked for that.

"She's a menace. Wait 'til I get my paws on her. You do not mess with a hellhound and walk away."

I lurched back as the cat sprang out of nowhere, and her back leg connected with Wiggles' jaw, sending him sprawling.

The cat bounced like a ninja to the other side of the store and landed neatly on her paws, her fur bristled around her like a big, fuzzy ginger mop, and her green eyes narrowed.

Wiggles jumped to his feet and shook his head. "That cat is going down."

"You scared her," I said.

"There's no need to thump me in the head with a dirty paw."

I studied the cat. This wasn't your typical moggy. She might not be a familiar, but power radiated off her. I shouldn't find it weird that animals had magic.

After all, I lived with a hellhound, and he was full of the stuff. But this cat felt unnaturally strong.

The cat sprung from the ground, launching herself at Wiggles again with an angry snarl.

He jumped out of the way and slammed into my legs, almost knocking me off balance.

I grabbed him off the ground and held him against my chest. "Stop annoying the poor pussycat."

"That thing is evil." Wiggles flipped around in my arms and flung his front paws over my shoulder. "What's wrong with her?"

"A nosy hellhound poked his snout at her, and she didn't appreciate it," I said.

"Oh! You find friend." Trixie Vermouth, our mayor's girlfriend, hurried over, her eyes widening as she looked at the furious cat who swiped her tail backward and forward.

"We didn't mean to annoy her," I said.

"Not your fault. This cat is mean." Trixie's accent was richly Eastern European, as were her dark looks. "She hate everybody."

"Why do you let her in?" I asked.

"We don't. She appears. Poof! Like magic. Mean cat. You leave now." Trixie opened the door and tried to usher the cat out.

The cat slunk onto her belly and glared at Trixie.

Trixie shook her head. She closed the door and popped the small rabbit she held into a cage. She'd worked here ever since coming to Willow Tree Falls, after meeting Mannie when they had a dalliance on a work trip. The dalliance continued, and he moved Trixie in with him.

"How's everything going here?" I asked.

"I love it," Trixie said. "I love animals, especially cute dogs." She booped Wiggles on the nose with a finger.

"And things are good with Mannie?" I asked.

"He's perfect," she said. "He treat me well."

"Still making lots of boom boom?" Wiggles asked.

I squeezed him to try to stop him from talking. "Ignore him. It's none of his business how much boom boom you make."

Trixie chuckled. "Yes, you naughty boy. Plenty of boom boom with my lusty dwarf. Excuse me. A customer needs me." She raced over to a woman who held a large grumpy silky gray cat.

"What do you think?" Aurora walked over with a small brown and black owl clamped to her shoulder. "This is Thaddeus."

My nose wrinkled. "I'm not sure an owl suits you."

Aurora nodded. "He's super sweet, but I'm not getting the vibe. I think he'd accept me, but I don't think it would be a strong bond. I want a familiar who'll stay with me for life. This owl doesn't seem all that committed. He might cheat on me."

The owl screeched and flapped his wings.

"What about that?" Wiggles gestured his head to the ground.

I looked over to see an enormous green toad hopping toward us with a determined look on his face.

"I'm not sure about a toad," Aurora said. "I mean, they're cute enough and clever. I worry someone might squish a toad if he gets out in the store when I'm busy. I'd be mortified to find my familiar dead under someone's shoe because they weren't looking where they were going."

"Stop doing that!" Abigail raced out of the back room and dumped a bag of cat food on the counter. "You can't let all the toads out."

I looked over to see a tall man with dark hair wearing a black suit delve into a glass case of toads. Several more toads escaped while he was prodding them.

"Grab those toads," Abigail yelled. "They're not cheap. I can't have them escaping."

I placed Wiggles down, and we herded the toads away from the door.

The owl on Aurora's shoulder swooped down and tried to grab a toad but was met by a warning blast of magic from Abigail.

"No, you don't, Thaddeus. No eating the other familiars. You know the rules," she said, her hands now full of toads.

Thaddeus flew up onto a high perch and screeched his annoyance at not getting a slimy snack.

"That's not the owl for you," I said to Aurora as I caught two toads in a plastic box. "Your familiar needs to be sweet-natured, not a killing machine."

Aurora peered into my box of toads. "The trouble is, I'm not sure what I want. Maybe I'm better off all alone."

Wiggles trotted over and dumped a toad into the box I held. "I'm definitely having doughnuts after this. These things don't taste good."

I glanced at the ginger cat who sat with her tail curled around her as she regarded the chaos. "Any time you want to help round up escaping toads, be my guest."

She flicked her tail, and it looked like a smirk crossed her furry face.

Abigail hurried over and took the box of toads from me. "Thank you for catching these."

"No problem." I glanced over her shoulder. "What was that guy up to letting them all out?"

"I've no idea," she said. "He claimed to be interested in the toads and wanted to try them all, but I don't believe him. I know when someone's ready for a familiar, just like your sister. He was a time waster. I sent him out the back, so he couldn't get near any more familiars and told him not to come back. No one messes with my babies and gets away with it."

"All the toads seem fine," I said. "I think we caught them all."

"Give me a second to put them in their home then we'll get back to finding your perfect familiar, Aurora." Abigail hurried away with the toads and placed them in the glass case.

Aurora studied Thaddeus on his perch. "Maybe a cat would be easier." She held her hand out to the ginger one. "Although, you've seen better days, sad kitty."

The cat swung her paw at Aurora's hand and caught the skin.

She jumped back and grabbed her bleeding hand. "I'm doomed. Even the familiars don't think I'm good enough for them."

"Oh, ignore that cat. She's grumpy with everyone." Abigail grabbed the ginger cat, opened the door, and shooed her out. She slammed the door in the cat's face before she had a chance to race back in. "She's definitely not for you. If she doesn't stop coming around, I'll have to find a more permanent solution for her."

"You won't have her put to sleep, will you?" Aurora's face paled. "She only scratched me."

"Oh, no. I mean, I'll get her put up for adoption or take her to a center for stray animals. I never put an unhealthy animal to sleep just because they don't behave themselves. Looking after all these familiars every day, I'm used to feisty behavior. Their powers make them a little self-important sometimes."

Aurora blew out a breath. "That's good to hear. But I think I've had enough familiar searching for now. I've ruled out toads and owls. Probably all birds and snakes."

"It takes time to find the right familiar," Abigail said. "Come back any time you like. You don't need to rush the process. When you're ready to find the perfect familiar, they'll be waiting for you."

Aurora thanked Abigail for her time, and we left the store.

Wiggles glanced around before heading into the street.

"What are you looking for?" I asked.

"I'm making sure that evil cat isn't waiting to pounce," he said. "My back stings from where she sliced me with her claws. I'll be scarred for life."

I did a quick search of his fur. "There are a few tiny pinpricks on your back. You'll be fine."

"You didn't have the beast land on you," he said. "Those claws hurt."

"She's gone now," I said.

"Let's go back to mine for hot chocolate," Aurora said, her expression glum, "unless you have somewhere better to go."

"No, I'm all yours. That sounds perfect." And maybe the hot chocolate would cheer her up.

We headed around the side of Heaven's Door and up the stairs to Aurora's apartment.

I sat on the stool by her white kitchen counter while Aurora made two hot chocolates covered in melting marshmallows and set out chocolate chip cookies.

Wiggles started begging as soon as he smelled the cookies.

I pulled out the chocolate chips and fed a cookie to him.

I couldn't ignore the miserable expression on my sister's face any longer. "What can I do to help?"

She slumped against the counter. "Have you got a time machine?"

I pursed my lips. "No can do. How about I erase your memories of Toby? It'll be like you never met him. You can forget how he turned you into a happy housewife and had you darning his socks."

She grimaced. "I don't think I darned his socks, but I do know he manipulated me."

"He manipulated all of us," I said. "That's his ability. You were just unfortunate he chose you to focus on."

"But he didn't," Aurora said, "not really. He only wanted me, so he could get to the demon prison and let them out. I feel such a fool."

"We all make mistakes," I said. "Maybe a memory erasing spell is just the thing you need. Forget your error and get on with your life."

Aurora sipped on her hot chocolate before shaking her head. "No, I needed to experience this. I always leap into a new relationship, thinking it will be perfect. I was always getting my hopes up and then being let down by guys who were too busy or not committed enough. This way, I've seen the very worst a relationship can offer."

"That's the spirit," I said. "Things can only get better. And you don't have to rush into anything next time. Take it slow. Have some fun."

"There may not be a next time," she said. "I'm serious about giving up on love."

"Not forever, though."

"No, I don't think I want to be alone forever," she said. "But for a while. I should stop looking so hard for my Mr. Right, and he might come to me. Isn't that what people always say happens?"

"Apparently so," I said.

"Besides, I can live my happy love life by watching you and Rhett."

"That sounds a bit creepy. What do you have in mind?"

"There's nothing creepy about it. Everything's good with you two, isn't it?"

"Sure, everything's great." Rhett and I kept it reasonably casual. We saw each other a couple of times a week and sometimes hung out at the weekends. It was good to have him by my side, but it never got too intense.

"It won't be much longer before you're engaged, and I can look forward to your wedding," Aurora said.

I choked on my hot chocolate and thumped my mug down. "Let's not get ahead of ourselves. Rhett's a great guy, but I'm not looking to get married anytime soon."

Her bottom lip jutted out. "I have to have something to look forward to."

"I can't get married just to make you happy," I said. "Don't jinx my relationship by putting pressure on us."

"You're right. I'm a relationship jinx. What's wrong with me?" Her chin wobbled.

"Nothing's wrong with you. You've just had some lousy luck. You're too trusting. Toby abused that." I passed her a cookie.

"I'm not trusting anyone ever again. It's just me and my shadow from now on."

"You love being in a couple. You'll find a decent guy soon enough."

She sighed, and her shoulders sagged.

I scooped the last of the marshmallows off my hot chocolate and sucked them off my finger. "Granny Dottie's idea of dating Tate isn't so bad. He's never looking for anything serious, he's great company, and you'd get all the free pizza you can manage."

Aurora tilted her head. "You really know how to sell a relationship. Although, free pizza isn't a terrible idea."

There was the old Aurora. "I can always put a good word in for you."

"Tempest orders from Tate at least twice a week. They're buddies," Wiggles said. "I bet he'd be happy to date you, Aurora."

"Thanks for the offer, but I'll stick to my hot chocolate and my broken heart for now," Aurora said.

There was only so much consoling I could do before my patience wore out. I finished my hot chocolate, grabbed another cookie, and stood. "I need to get going. Cloven Hoof will be opening in a couple of hours. You should drop by. Your Mr. Right might be hanging out at the bar."

Aurora stuffed a cookie in her mouth. "No thanks."

That was it, sympathy quotient drained.

We said our goodbyes, and I headed out the store with Wiggles.

I needed to get Aurora fixed up quickly. If I didn't, she'd fixate on my romance with Rhett. We were happy just as we were. Our relationship was great, but marriage. Eek! That was way too scary to contemplate.

Operation Find Aurora a New Boyfriend was on.

Chapter 3

"Croissant, bear claw, or Danish pastry?" I pulled on my jacket and grabbed my keys.

Wiggles bounced around in the apartment. "Decisions, decisions."

All I wanted was an extra strong coffee. It had been a late night at Cloven Hoof, and I hadn't rolled into bed until past three that morning.

"I'm considering a croissant," I said.

"I'll have all three." Wiggles bounced down the stairs in front of me.

"Not if you want to keep your sylphlike figure," I said.

"I can handle a few extra rolls if it means I have a bear claw every morning."

The sun was high in the sky as we headed toward Sprinkles. I'd planned a long, relaxing day of doing nothing. I'd over-indulge on pastries, drink too much coffee, and maybe do a little browsing around the stores before heading back home for some more sleep.

Wiggles froze to the spot, and the fur on his back lifted.

"What's wrong with you?" I asked.

"I spot evil at fifty paces."

"Evil?" Had a demon gotten loose from the prison?

"It's that cat again," he hissed.

I laughed as I spotted the grubby ginger cat from Abigail's store. "She's hardly evil."

Wiggles lifted his nose. "Do you smell that?"

"No! And stop mentioning her smell. I bet she can hear you. You know what happened yesterday when you insulted her."

"It's not dirty cat stink. I smell blood."

My eyes widened as I stared at the cat. I walked closer. Wiggles was right. Her paws were covered in dried blood.

The cat's gaze lasered on to us as we drew nearer.

I lifted a hand. "Hey, we don't mean any harm. Have you been hurt?"

The cat's tail swished, but she didn't move.

My gaze ran over her slowly. I couldn't see any injuries that had caused the blood on her paws. It looked like she'd been standing in the stuff.

Wiggles remained behind me. "I bet that's the blood of her latest victim."

The cat sounded like she was coughing up a hair ball. Although, when I listened closely, it almost sounded like laughter.

"Did something happen?" I glanced around. It wasn't so weird to be seen talking to animals in this village, but I didn't want to be spotted by too many people talking to a cat.

The cat stood and turned away from us, flicking her tail in the air.

"I told you," Wiggles whispered. "She's evil. Don't trust her."

"Can you show us where you got that blood on your paws?" I asked the cat.

She glanced over her shoulder and continued walking.

"What do you reckon?" I asked Wiggles. "Should we follow?"

"Absolutely not. I have a bear claw with my name on it."

"Five minutes," I said.

"Then I get two bear claws. Three if that cat attacks me again."

"Fine. But I want to know where that blood came from."

Wiggles grumbled before walking along with me. "I have a bad feeling in my gut."

"More trapped wind?"

He snorted. "That cat is trouble."

I had the same uneasy feeling. There was something different about this cat.

We followed her for several minutes until she turned right and headed along an alleyway.

"You don't wanna go down there," Wiggles said. "Nothing good ever happens in dark alleyways."

"It's the middle of the day," I said. "What she going to do?"

"Kill us and stuff our bodies in a trash can?"

"You sound scared," I said. "Did the cute kitten terrify you yesterday?"

Wiggles grumbled and stamped along beside me. "I'm not scared of anybody."

The cat stopped by an open door and pulled it wider with her paw before sliding inside.

I hurried after her and saw a sign by the door. We were at the back entrance to Fur Baby Emporium.

I poked my head in and looked around. There was a short corridor and two doors off either side. The cat stopped by one and looked back at me.

"Let's see what this cat's been up to," I said.

"I reckon she's slaughtered an entire knot of toads," he said, "or maybe an owl."

I followed the cat and opened the door. She raced right through. I pulled up short as Abigail appeared with a box in her hands.

She jumped, and the box fell to the ground. "Oh! You scared me, Tempest! What are you doing here? This area is for employees only."

I pushed the door open wider. "I was following that cat." I pointed to the ginger kitty who watched us from a short distance away.

Abigail grabbed the box and piled the wrapped items back in. "She's back again?"

"Yes, and take a closer look," I said. "There's something on her paws."

"It's blood," Wiggles blurted out as he barged past me. "That cat's up to something. She led us here. Has she eaten all your toads?"

The cat hissed at Wiggles.

Abigail placed the box down and kicked it carefully to one side. "It does look like blood. Where's it from?"

The cat disappeared to the back of the store room.

"I'm not sure, which is why we followed her." I continued tailing the cat, Wiggles and Abigail not far behind. "You have a lot of stock."

"I bulk buy," Abigail said. "You get a better discount that way. I've just had a delivery come in and was sorting through it. It's not usually this cluttered."

I edged past a head-high pile of boxes and found the cat waiting.

She turned and continued, rounding the corner at the back of the store room.

An unpleasant metallic tang filled the air. We were about to discover where the cat had found the blood.

I turned the corner and stopped. Lying behind a pile of boxes was the body of a man.

Wiggles joined me and stared at the body. "Huh! Who's that?"

"Have you found something?" Abigail hurried to join us. She gasped as she peered over my shoulder. "Oh my. Not in my store." She staggered backward and fainted to the floor.

I glanced at her and shook my head.

"Isn't that the toad guy?" Wiggles asked. "The guy from the store who was messing with Abigail's familiars."

I leaned over him, trying to ignore his sightless eyes. "You're right." I stepped back and looked around. There were bloody cat pawprints all over the place.

The ginger cat sat to one side, staring solemnly at the body.

"What's going on here?" I asked the cat. "Did you find the body like this?" I didn't know why I was asking her. It wasn't as if the cat could talk.

Wiggles stared at the body and snorted. "He's not dead."

"He looks very dead to me," I said.

"No! He's moving. Look at his chest." He jabbed a paw at the body.

I stared intently. The man's chest was definitely writhing, but it wasn't rising and falling as if he was breathing.

"Check for a pulse," Wiggles said.

"You check for a pulse!" I said. "Look at his face. His eyes are open, and his skin is gray. That guy isn't alive!"

"Well, there's something freaky going on with him." Wiggles inched closer to the body. He bounced back and slammed into my legs. "He is moving!"

I gritted my teeth and edged nearer, keeping Wiggles by my side. I reached forward slowly and touched his neck. As expected, there was no pulse.

"You don't think..." Wiggles stared at the guy's chest. "I mean, he's in a store full of familiars. What if some of them got out and are enjoying a feast?"

I swallowed my revulsion. "That's for Abigail to deal with. Or the angels. Let's not get involved. We don't know this guy, and the angels hate us poking about."

"What if my theory's right, and this evil cat killed him?" he said. "We've already found the killer. Case solved."

The cat's fur bristled, and she growled.

"It's not the cat. She might have ninja moves, but she couldn't inflict that." I pointed at the head wound.

There was a rush of movement, and I fell back as enormous fangs clamped around my arm. Cool scales wrapped around my wrist, and the fangs bit in deeper.

"Arrgghhh! Get it off me!" I staggered as an enormous python wrapped around me.

"That's what was eating the body," Wiggles yelled. "That's Goliath."

"I don't care what his name is! He's eating me now. Blast your fire at him." Hot shards of pain raced up my arm as the fangs sliced through all kinds of important things I didn't want to think about.

The cat made that coughing laugh again. The evil little thing was enjoying this.

I didn't have time to care as the circulation was cut off in my hand as the snake continued to wrap itself around me. It was like being trapped in a vice, one that was going to squish me to death and then have a feast on my remains.

"I can't blast you," Wiggles said as he danced around me, nipping at the snake's tail. "You'll burn."

"Burns I can handle; being swallowed by this enormous beast isn't an option."

Wiggles blasted fire, but the snake was fast and lunged away, taking me with it.

"Abigail! I'm being eaten by your snake. Wake up!" I battled with the snake, grabbing its powerful jaw with my free hand and trying to prise it open. That hurt way too much, and I almost fainted from the pain.

All the while, Abigail remained unhelpfully passed out on the floor.

"You'd better let go of me," I warned the snake. "I've been looking for a new pair of boots. Don't make me think about investing in some snakeskin ones."

The snake blinked once, and its hold on me lessened.

I conjured a lightning spell and held it over the snake's head. "This will hurt both of us, but I'll unleash this spell unless you drop my arm right now."

The fangs retracted an inch, and I winced as a throbbing pulse of pain shot up my arm.

"Final warning." I swallowed my terror. "Snakeskin boots for you."

The snake uncurled in a rapid pulse of energy, and the fangs vanished from my arm.

I let out a shaky sigh as the snake slithered away, and I was left with a bleeding arm and a circle of bruises lacing from my wrist up to my shoulder.

I looked at the body on the floor, the smug cat, the retreating form of the snake, and finally Abigail. Something super freaky had gone down here.

My breath came out shaky. "Wiggles, I hate to say it, but we'd better let the angels take a look at this mess."

Chapter 4

I was rubbing a healing salve I'd found in Abigail's medicine cabinet on my bite wounds when the door to Fur Baby Emporium opened.

"Tempest?" It was Dazielle, head of Angel Force.

"Back here," I called, holding my still throbbing arm against my chest. "Keep the door closed. There's an enormous witch eating snake on the loose, and he's not afraid to use his fangs when he gets disturbed."

Dazielle's wings fluttered out around her as she entered the back of the store and took in the devastation. She was accompanied by Dominic, secretly my favorite angel, and Cassiel, definitely not my favorite angel.

"Dominic, wait by the door. Look out for that snake," she said. "Cassiel, you're with me." The two angels strode toward me.

I sucked in a breath, knowing exactly what was about to happen.

"What have you done?" Dazielle crossed her arms over her chest.

"I told you that cat would get us in trouble," Wiggles muttered.

"I'm innocent in all of this," I said. "I found a cat outside with blood on her paws. She led us here. And—"

"Hold on. You followed a random cat into the store?" Dazielle arched an eyebrow. "Why would you do that?"

"Let's just say we have history with this cat," I said. "We came to the store yesterday to find a familiar for Aurora. We met this cat, and she fought with Wiggles."

"I almost beat her," Wiggles said. "I would have, but she surprised me. She fights dirty."

"Go on," Dazielle said. "What happened today to bring you here?"

"The cat turned up just as we were leaving Cloven Hoof to get lunch. Well, breakfast. Brunch, I guess," I said. "I thought she'd been injured, but she led us here, and we found the body."

"Who is it?" Dazielle asked.

"No idea. He's not from around here. Although, he was also in the store yesterday. It looks like someone's whacked him over the head."

"And what does the killer snake have to do with this?" Dazielle peered at the body.

"I really don't know," I said. "The snake was wrapped around the body. When I checked for a pulse, I guess he took offense and did this." I held up my damaged arm.

Abigail groaned and lifted a hand.

"See to her," Dazielle said to Cassiel. "Why did you knock out Abigail?"

I scowled at her. "Not guilty. She took one look at the dead guy and fainted."

She arched an eyebrow and moved closer to the body. "He doesn't look familiar."

"All I know is that he was causing Abigail trouble yesterday. He let a load of her familiars out in the store. Abigail sent him away after that. She wasn't impressed."

Dazielle's lips pursed. "Perhaps he came back and caused her more trouble. Trouble enough that she decided to get rid of him for good."

My eyes widened. That was a big leap. "You think Abigail killed the guy because he let her toads loose? That's not the best motive I've ever heard."

"What happened?" Abigail's voice was weak as Cassiel helped her to sit up.

I glanced around Dazielle, whose wings obscured my sightline. "Remember the dead body?"

She rubbed her head. "Oh dear. That really happened?"

"Do you know this man?" Dazielle asked as she approached Abigail.

"No. I mean, not really." Abigail stood slowly, helped by Cassiel. "He was here yesterday. He spent about an hour looking around but didn't buy anything."

"Is that unusual?" Dazielle asked.

"Not really," she said. "It takes people many visits before they find their perfect familiar. But I could tell he wasn't serious. Some people come here because they like to look at the familiars, and that's fine, but he was a time waster. And then he started causing problems with my toads. I had to get rid of him."

"Quite literally by the look of things," Dazielle said.

Abigail blinked at her several times. "What do you mean by that?"

"I mean, you have a dead body in your store. How did he wind up here if you're not involved?"

"I have no idea," Abigail said. "I've been sorting new stock most of the morning and haven't been back here. What happened to him?"

"He was murdered," Wiggles said. "If you're looking for who did it, I blame that cat."

The cat who'd been watching everything in silent contemplation hissed at Wiggles.

"Really? A cat?" Dazielle shook her head. "I'm not buying that."

"I know it sounds odd, but I was telling the truth about the cat bringing us here," I said. "She knows something about this murder. I'm not saying she did it, but she might have seen something."

"You're suggesting I interrogate the cat?" Dazielle sighed. "Cassiel, secure the scene and deal with the body. Abigail, we'll need to speak to you back at the station."

"I can't leave the store," she said. "I'm on my own today."

"Can't Trixie come in?" I asked.

"Maybe, it's her day off. I'll have to check. I can't close the store. The familiars need taking care of. They get stressed if they're left alone during the day."

"We'll be here for a while," Dazielle said. "Make whatever arrangements you need, but no one can come in here until we've checked for evidence."

"What about my customers?" Abigail asked. "I hate letting them down."

"Abigail, someone was murdered in your store," Dazielle said. "You'll have to accept you're going to miss a day of trading, so we can find evidence to lead us to the killer."

"Oh, very well." Abigail huffed out a breath. "I'll put a note up to say I'm closed for a stock take."

"What about that cat?" Wiggles said. "She knows evil things. You should at least check her for evidence."

Dazielle lifted her gaze to the ceiling. "Cassiel, get the cat."

Cassiel's lips pursed. "Is that necessary?"

"Most likely not, but she is covered in evidence. Look at those bloody paws," Dazielle said.

Cassiel frowned as she made a half-hearted grab for the cat.

She darted away from Cassiel with an angry shriek and raced out the back door before anybody could stop her.

"You just let a killer go!" Wiggles said.

I wasn't sure the cat had killed this stranger, but she knew what was going on. There was more to that furball than a cute meow.

"Let's forget the cat for now," Dazielle said. "Abigail, is there anything else you can tell me about the victim?"

She sniffed. "He had no manners. He was rude and suggested my familiars were substandard. He wasn't welcome back here."

"Why is he in your store room if you didn't want him back?" Dazielle asked.

She shook her head. "I didn't realize he was here until Tempest came through the back and spotted him."

Dazielle's gaze shifted to me. "What were you doing sneaking around the back of this store?"

"I wasn't sneaking. I followed the cat."

Dazielle's eyebrow arched. "For any particular reason?"

I felt ridiculous admitting that the cat understood me when I asked her questions. "I thought she might be injured. She had blood on her fur. The cat led us along this alleyway and came through the open back door. That's when we found the body."

Dazielle's mouth twisted to the side. "Very well. Let's see who we've got here." She approached the body and checked his pockets before pulling out a wallet. She flipped it open.

I craned to look around her, but she tilted the wallet, so I couldn't see.

"Well? Who is it?" I asked.

"John Smith." Dazielle sighed. "Not helpful. That's a common name in this country."

"You don't think it's his real name?" I asked.

She shrugged. "It could be. There's nothing remarkable inside his wallet. He's definitely not a local."

"I haven't seen him before," I said. "We could check at the hotel to see if he's booked a room."

Dazielle shook her head. "*We* aren't going to do anything. I don't want you nosing around in this."

"I wasn't planning to," I said. "If I hadn't been attacked by that giant snake while checking to see if John was even alive, we'd be long gone by now."

"Oh! Goliath." Abigail looked around. "What happened to him? You must have scared him. He never attacks. He's a big placid baby."

"I must have caught him on a bad day." I gently squeezed my throbbing arm.

"He's a sweetie." Abigail ducked and began searching for the snake.

"You should leave him alone to calm down," I said. "Those fangs pack a punch. The fact I'm still alive makes me think he has no venom in those giant fangs."

"No, they're just to trap prey. I can see him under here." Abigail crawled along a row of shelving as she peered underneath it. "Goliath, come out of there. We're not angry with you."

"I am," I muttered.

"I can reach him." Abigail lay flat on the ground and shoved her hand under the shelving.

She was a braver woman than me. I had no plans to go near that snake ever again.

"I've almost got his tail," she said.

"Is she crazy?" Wiggles muttered. "That snake almost ate you."

I shrugged. It was Abigail's snake. Maybe they had a bond.

"Let's leave the giant, angry snake for now." Dazielle eyed the shelving cautiously. "We don't want to irritate him if he's already unhappy."

"He'll be fine once I reach him," Abigail said. "He might be scared. Familiars react badly to stress."

"He's the scared one?" Wiggles said.

"Almost got him." Abigail was now half underneath the shelving. "I think—" She shrieked, and her hair stood on end as her body shook.

I grabbed her leg and yanked her backward, thinking she was being eaten by Goliath. A shiver of magic danced across my skin before vanishing. I flipped Abigail onto her back. Her eyes were wide, and she looked frozen.

"Did the snake do that?" Dazielle peered at Abigail, alarm in her eyes.

"No, it was the magic bound to the snake that made Abigail freak out." I pressed a hand to Abigail's cheek, and she let out a huge gasp of air.

I glanced up to see Goliath's scaly head poking out from under the shelving. "Stay where you are, buddy. No one wants any more of your snaky action. Keep those fangs to yourself."

He looked almost shamefaced as he slowly slithered away toward his glass case, his huge muscular body contracting and expanding as he moved.

Abigail drew in another shuddering breath and blinked at me. "He's been be-spelled. The second I touched his skin, whatever was controlling him shifted up my arm. That's why he behaved so oddly with you. Someone has used my beautiful Goliath for this foul deed."

"Whoever killed this guy must have used the snake to trap him," I said. "They put a spell on Goliath, so he'd act like a guard snake."

"Are you suggesting I take the snake into custody as a possible accomplice to this murder?" Dazielle asked.

"It's not a terrible idea," I said. "Goliath most likely saw everything. He could be your only witness in this murder."

Dazielle sighed. "Get out of here, Tempest. We'll handle things."

I raised my hands. "Fine by me." I had no desire to be involved in the angels' business any longer than necessary.

Abigail shuffled upright. "Poor Goliath. He's one of my favorites. Don't hold it against him. He's not involved in this. Someone mistreated him and forced him to behave badly."

I didn't mind snakes but was never going to be their biggest fan after one just sunk their huge fangs into my arm. "Whatever that magic was, you released it when you touched him. It had a dark bite to it, and I'm not talking about those killer fangs."

"Yes! I felt that too. Whoever used magic on my baby boy isn't a gentle magic user."

"It's someone with a dark vibe." I tapped my chin. "Someone living in the village?"

"Tempest," Dazielle said sharply. "That's enough. We're looking after this investigation. Your help is not needed or wanted."

"Well, since that's the case, I'll leave you to it." I nodded goodbye to Abigail and headed out the back door with Wiggles.

I was happy to let the angels deal with this mess. Besides, I had a cat I wanted to chat to. Those bloody paws were involved in this, somehow.

I'd figure out exactly what that sneaky puss had been up to in the store room of Fur Baby Emporium.

Chapter 5

"We could try memory extraction spells." I was hunting in another alleyway, looking for the elusive, bloody-pawed cat who'd raced out of Fur Baby Emporium.

"Will that work on a familiar?" Wiggles asked.

"We don't know this cat is a familiar, but she's something with power," I said.

We'd been searching all afternoon and had only stopped for a couple of bear claws and a huge mug of coffee before continuing our search of the whole village. So far, there was no sign of the cat.

"That cat didn't seem too clever to me," Wiggles said. "Any memories you extract will be garbled and full of obsessions about chasing feathers and figuring out how to cough up the grossest hairball."

"We should try a memory extraction on the snake," I said. "Although, there's no way I'm getting close to him again." My arm still throbbed, despite using two healing spells and salve.

I dropped a cardboard box I'd moved and sighed. We'd looked everywhere. The cat was gone.

"The angels can handle that snake." Wiggles shuddered. "We don't ever need to see Goliath again."

"But someone has been manipulating Abigail's familiars," I said. "It could be that this cat is also involved. Our encounters with her suggest she's not your average cat."

"That makes sense," Wiggles said. "It must be the reason she beat me."

I suppressed a laugh. "You'd never be bested by a normal pussycat."

He snorted a cloud of sulfur rich smoke. "Exactly. I can't smell her anymore. The trail has gone cold."

"Let's grab a late lunch and head back to Cloven Hoof." We were all out of places to look. My feet ached, and I needed a sit down with a big plate of chocolate brownies.

So far, my relaxing day of doing nothing had been scuppered by finding a cat with bloody paws and a dead body. Still, I had the remains of the afternoon. It didn't need to be a complete write-off.

"Pizza?" Wiggles asked.

I grinned. "What else?"

We headed to Mystic Mushroom, grabbed an extra-large meat feast with a side order of garlic bread, and strolled back to the club.

I slowed, and my eyes narrowed. Sitting outside the doors of the club was the cat.

"You have got to be kidding me. All this time we've been looking for you, and you've been right here." I stomped toward the cat.

She lifted her gaze and tilted her head. Amusement glittered in her green eyes.

"She looks smug," Wiggles said. "I bet she was watching us look for her the whole time."

I opened the door and glared at the cat. "Are you coming in?"

The cat stared at the door for several seconds before hopping up and trotting inside.

Not that I needed it confirmed, but it proved this cat had something magical about her. Only individuals with magic could walk through the doors of Cloven Hoof.

I smiled as Wiggles kept a wide gap between him and the cat. His ego was still a little bruised by being bested by her.

We headed upstairs to the apartment, and the cat seemed perfectly content to come inside. She sniffed around for a minute and then turned and sat, curling her tail around her paws and studying me with a calm expression on her furry face.

I dished out the pizza for Wiggles and me.

"Do you eat pizza?" I asked the cat.

Her nose wrinkled.

"Don't waste good pizza on her," Wiggles said.

"Don't be so mean," I said. "She's skinny. She must be hungry. How about some dog kibble?"

Her wrinkled nose became even more pronounced, and her green eyes narrowed.

I hunted in the fridge and pulled out a slice of roast chicken.

"Hey! You never give me roast chicken," Wiggles said.

"That's because you're on a strict diet," I said. It mainly consisted of sugary pastries, pizza, and anything he could find in the trash.

Wiggles swallowed his huge mouthful of pizza. "Don't go getting any ideas that you're keeping this cat. There's only room for one animal in your life. The position's filled. No cats allowed."

"The thought hadn't crossed my mind." I held the chicken out to the cat.

She sniffed it, turned her large eyes to me, and blinked.

"A cat who doesn't like chicken," I said. "You're definitely not your normal kitty cat, are you?"

The cat hopped onto the counter and placed her paws on the edge of the fruit bowl. There was a wrinkled apple, two overripe bananas, and a couple of shriveled grapes at the bottom.

My eyebrows rose as she dabbed a paw at the apple. "You want fruit?"

The cat meowed.

I grabbed the wrinkled apple and cut off a small piece before giving it to her.

She gobbled it down.

"Huh! She's into fruit," Wiggles said. "I guess she does have a use."

I cut up half the apple and placed it on a plate on the floor.

The cat got to work polishing off the fruit.

"What sort of cat is this?" I watched her crunch her way through the apple.

"An awful one," Wiggles said. "Any animal who likes fruit more than a large slice of pizza has to have something wrong with it."

I finished my own pizza and wiped my hands clean before grabbing a spell book off the shelf. "Let's try a little memory spell on her. If we extract anything useful, we can find out who John Smith really is and what he was doing sneaking around the back of Abigail's store."

"I thought we were leaving this to the angels," Wiggles said.

"We are. I'm just curious."

The cat looked at the spell book and then at me.

"Don't worry. This won't hurt." I checked through the spell details and touched the tip of my finger to the cat's head. Nothing happened.

I tried again. "That's weird. Something's blocking me."

"You're trying magic on a beast with low intelligence," Wiggles said. "There's not much going on behind those evil green eyes."

The cat narrowed her eyes and glowered at him.

"There's something there," I said. "She understands us." I attempted another memory spell, but it failed to have any effect.

I flicked through the pages of the spell book, looking for something with a little more power.

The cat strode over and batted my fingers with a soft paw.

"You have a better idea?" I asked her.

She stared at the book and flicked at the pages.

I flipped it to the contents page and turned it to her. "What would you choose?"

She stared at the page for several seconds before pressing her nose to a spell.

"A speech spell!"

"That won't work," Wiggles said. "That cat won't be able to talk. Not smart enough."

"I'm willing to try anything," I said. "Okay, kitty. Let's see what you've got to tell us." I rested my fingers on her head. The magic pulsed through me, and the hairs on my arms stood on end as the spell took hold.

The cat slowly backed away, her body shaking as her fur bristled.

"Careful," Wiggles said. "She's about to explode. We don't want kitty guts all over the walls."

The shaking subsided. The cat shook her head, and it sounded like she cleared her throat.

"Did it work?" I asked her. "Can you talk?"

She coughed again. "You need to run me a bath. My fur smells of death and hellhound."

Chapter 6

My jaw dropped. She was the poshest cat I'd ever heard. Well, she was the only cat I'd ever heard talk. "Wow! That's... interesting."

The cat settled on the counter, and her eyes narrowed as she looked at Wiggles. "I do not like dogs."

"Good news, furball. I'm a hellhound." He bared his teeth.

The posh cat lifted her nose. "Even worse."

A growl rumbled from Wiggles' chest.

"Easy now. This cat is a guest," I said. "What's your name, puss?"

She glanced at me. "Bandit."

"Dumb name," Wiggles muttered.

"Dumb hellhound," she shot back.

"She can't stay," he said. "The cat leaves."

I lifted a hand. "She may have useful information."

"The only use she has is eating fruit," he said.

I raised my eyebrows. "Okay, Bandit. Let's start at the beginning. What are you doing in Willow Tree Falls?"

She shook her head. "I insist on a bath before anything else. Run me one, witch. All I can smell is that dead man's blood on my feet."

"You want a bath?" I asked. "Don't cats hate water?"

"As you must have gathered by now, I'm a little more than your average house cat."

"Yeah, you're a massive pain in the behind," Wiggles muttered.

She hissed at him. "I'm not afraid to put you in your place again, mutt."

"I'd like to see you try." Wiggles scrambled to get on the countertop.

I scooped him up and set him on the floor before putting the remains of the pizza next to him as a distraction. "If I run you a bath, will you talk?" I asked Bandit.

"I'll tell you what I know, which isn't much."

"Fair enough." I walked into the bathroom and ran the water until it grew hot. "Do you want bubbles?" I glanced over my shoulder to see the cat standing in the doorway.

"Of course. None of the cheap stuff. It irritates my skin." She scratched behind her ear with a back paw.

I sorted through several of the open bottles of bubble bath on the shelf before selecting one with a pungent jasmine scent. I tipped some in the water and swirled it around until it foamed.

I shut off the faucet and settled on the closed toilet lid. "Ready when you are."

Bandit peered over the edge of the bath. "That looks acceptable." She hopped on the edge, balancing for a second before leaping straight in.

She vanished under the water before her head popped up, covered in bubbles.

She swam around for a couple of laps before letting out a sigh. "That already feels so much better. Bathing with your tongue does not get you clean. I can't figure out why cats spend so much time licking themselves."

"It's a tough life. So, what exactly are you if you're not your average cat?"

She did another lap of the bath. "A be-spelled fairy."

"A fairy!"

"A mean one," Wiggles shouted from the living room.

Fairies could be mean. Some were sparkly and fun, but many had dark sides. There was truth to the myths about them stealing children while they slept.

"Is your name really Bandit?" I asked.

"No. I picked it as my cat name."

"What's your fairy name?"

She glanced at me. "I forget."

"When were you changed into a cat?"

"My memory's muddled. I find myself increasingly thinking about chasing my tail." She stopped swimming. "I believe it was around a month ago."

"Who be-spelled you?" I asked.

"The dead man," she said. "At least, that's the last clear memory I have. We were arguing about something, I don't remember what. The next thing I remember is becoming this furry creature obsessed with chattering at birds and chasing anything that moves."

"John Smith was a powerful magic user?"

"He must have had power," Bandit said. "I don't get fooled easily."

"How did you know the victim?"

"I can't tell you. I do remember he wasn't a nice man."

"How did you come to be in Willow Tree Falls?"

"I was following him," Bandit said. "I was determined to get him to remove this spell and change me back."

"He changed you before you came here?"

"Yes, he only arrived a few days ago."

I rubbed my chin. "Now he's dead, and the spell remains in place? When a person dies, their magic usually breaks. You shouldn't still be a cat."

"I'm hoping it will fade in time," Bandit said. "But so far, I still feel very catlike."

"You really can't recall why he turned you into a cat? You must have done something to annoy him."

"That's likely." Wiggles wandered into the bathroom.

"Do you mind?" Bandit kicked the soap at Wiggles. "There's a lady in the bath."

"You have your clothes on," Wiggles said, "well, your fur."

"Even so, it's not polite for some smelly old hound to come in and interfere."

Wiggles settled on the floor. "I'm staying put. This is my bathroom."

Bandit scowled at him.

"It sounds like you had a connection to John Smith," I said. "Not a positive one. Did you kill him?"

Bandit rested her front paws on the edge of the bath. "With these pathetic things? Hardly likely."

"But you must still have magic," I said. "You understood us when we talked to you. Can you still do spells in your cat form?"

"Very little," she said. "A few basic spells, but nothing that would kill a person."

"What about Goliath, the snake?" I asked. "Did you make him act oddly? What was he doing wrapped around John when we found him?"

"I can't answer that," Bandit said. "All I can tell you is that I snuck through the cat flap in Abigail's back door, following a weird smell. She often leaves food out in the store. I've been sneaking in for a while now to get something to eat, although she tends to leave out animal food."

I nodded slowly. "You prefer fruit?"

"Absolutely. I barely tolerate that disgusting kibble she puts down, but if there's nothing else going, I have no choice. I only eat fruit, green things, and anything brown, so chocolate brownies count. Basically, anything colored the same as nature, just like all fairies. It's good for you. In fact, I'll have more fruit."

I glanced at Wiggles. "Go grab that banana from the fruit bowl."

He shook his head. "I'm not her slave."

"No, but we're getting useful information." I didn't want to leave Bandit whilst she was talking. I also wasn't prepared to leave them on their own in case Wiggles jumped in the tub and tried to drown her.

"I grow weak with hunger," Bandit said. "Get my food, hound."

He growled at her before stomping out of the bathroom. He returned a few seconds later and spat the whole banana into the bath.

She flicked water at him. "Heathen. Peel it for me."

"Peel your own banana," he said.

I scooped the banana out of the bubbles and unpeeled it before placing a small piece on the edge of the bath.

Bandit gobbled it down.

"So, you got into the store. Then what?" I placed more banana down for Bandit.

"I found John dead on the floor."

"Why were your paw prints everywhere?"

"I'd looked around. It was dark when I got in there. I could smell something was off, but I had to leap up the wall to flick on the lights. That's when I realized I'd been standing in his blood as I walked around."

"Did you see anyone else there?"

"I was alone. I ran off when I heard Abigail come into the store. That's when I saw you coming out of Cloven Hoof. I remembered seeing you in the store yesterday."

"Did you see anything odd about the body?" I asked.

"Other than the snake wrapped around him?"

"Yeah, that is weird. Forget the snake for a second. John was dead when you found him?" I asked.

"Yes, the body was already cold. He'd been dead for hours, and the blood I'd been stamping around in was congealing," Bandit said.

My nose wrinkled. "So, who was he? Why did someone kill him in Abigail's store?"

"No clue," Bandit said. "I've been hanging around her store for a while, and the only time I saw him in there was the day he set the toads loose."

"Is it a coincidence John ended up dead in the back of Abigail's store room?" I asked. "She seemed genuinely shocked at seeing him."

"I never figured Abigail for a killer," Wiggles said.

"Same here. Maybe it was her bad luck he stumbled through the door and died there. He could have been injured in the alleyway and was trying to find somewhere to hide from his actual killer. Or was he looking for help because he'd been injured," I said.

"Check my paws are clean of blood." Bandit grabbed my loofah from the side of the bath with her teeth and flipped over, balancing her head on it as she stuck her paws in the air.

I gave her paws a quick look over. "All good."

"You may shampoo me now," Bandit said.

I snorted a laugh. "This isn't a pet parlor."

"I still smell funny," she said. "You don't know how difficult it is to stay clean while wearing fur."

"I'll do it, so long as you keep talking." I grabbed a bar of soap.

"No! Not soap, witch. Shampoo my fur and then deep condition it." Bandit sighed and shook her head.

I grumbled under my breath as I opened my coconut shampoo. "Anything else, milady?"

"A paw massage afterwards will be acceptable."

"No paw massage," Wiggles grumbled. "Only I get my paws massaged."

I bit back a laugh as I scooped Bandit out and thoroughly shampooed her. She really was filthy. I felt a bit sorry for the fairy cat. She might be a bit snooty, but it must be a shock having to adjust to life as a cat after spending your days as an airborne fairy, sprinkling magical, sparkly dust and stealing children.

"Have you seen John with anyone else while he's been in Willow Tree Falls?" I asked.

"He only arrived a few days ago," Bandit said. "I'd tracked his movements but kept getting distracted. You see, I have a fascination with feathers. Those angels are of particular interest. I bet they taste amazing."

Wiggles snorted. "You wanna chase an angel, be my guest. That would be fun to watch."

"Best not," I said. "So, you didn't stick with John all the time?"

"No. I lost him several times, and he'd vanish for hours. Although, I saw him arguing with somebody on the street the day he died."

"What were they arguing about?"

"I wasn't close enough to hear, but it was heated. They were yelling in each other's faces. It looked like they might come to blows."

"Who was it?" I asked.

"I didn't recognize the woman, but he yelled her name as she walked away. He shouted Raine."

My gut clenched. "Are you sure?"

"Absolutely." Bandit tilted her head as she looked at me. "She looked a bit like you, actually. Same hair color, dark clothes, and a similar surly expression."

"I don't have a surly expression. This is just my face," I said. "Are you certain he said Raine?"

"I am. Why? Do you know somebody called Raine?" Bandit asked. "Is she a bad sort?"

I bit my lip as I rinsed shampoo out of Bandit's fur. What was my cousin doing arguing with a man who'd just been murdered?

Chapter 7

Cloven Hoof was busy, but I still spotted Raine and Azura when they arrived.

After getting everything I could out of Bandit during her bath time, I needed to speak to Raine about how she knew the dead guy and what they'd been fighting about the day he was killed.

I waved them over to the bar. "Wiggles, you need to distract Azura. I have to get Raine on her own, so I can quiz her."

Wiggles stopped snuffling on the floor behind the bar and nodded. "Leave it to me. I'll show her my new tricks."

"What new tricks?"

"I'll make some up. I can show her some paw stands, and maybe I'll jump through fire. That should keep her entertained."

"Yeah, sounds good. Just try not to burn the place down when you do that."

"Hey, Tempest." Raine stopped by the bar. "Thanks for the invite."

"No problem," I said. "Happy to have you both here. What can I get you?"

"We'll have two double shots of lemon drops and..." Azura looked down the menu. "Two bowls of your dried Tibetan mushrooms. They sound good."

"Coming right up." I nodded at Wiggles.

He bounded around the bar. "Azura, come see my tricks. I do this amazing thing with fire."

She grinned. "Show us then."

"Not here," he said. "Tempest told me I can't singe the customers. She's no fun. Come out the back." Wiggles was bouncing on his paws and circling Azura.

"Okay, five minutes," Azura said. "I really want my lemon drop, though."

Raine went to follow them, but I grabbed her elbow. "Did you hear about what happened at Abigail's store?"

She shook her head. "No. What's up?"

"Someone was found dead in her store room this morning."

Raine's eyebrows shot up, and she settled on a stool. "No kidding. Who was it?"

"No one local." I watched her closely. "Apparently, his name is John Smith."

She nodded, showing no sign she knew the guy. "What happened?"

"Not sure. The angels are investigating."

"So, we'll never find out if they're looking into it." She smirked and took a sip of her lemon drop.

"Actually, I found the body," I said. "And the weird thing was, there was a snake wrapped around him."

"That is weird," Raine said.

"You don't know him?" I asked.

"Why would I know this dead guy?" She glanced around the club.

"I just wondered if you'd seen him around Willow Tree Falls. Tall, kind of handsome if you like the neat type, wearing a dark suit."

"Can't say I have." She took another sip of her drink.

"So, you weren't arguing with him just before he died?"

Raine jerked back in her seat. "What makes you say that?"

I leaned across the bar. "Someone saw you with him. I'm just trying to find out what happened."

She shrugged. "Whoever saw that is mistaken."

My heart raced. Raine was hiding something. "Apparently, you were heard yelling at him. Why were you yelling at the dead guy?"

"You're wrong." She downed the rest of her lemon drop and grabbed a handful of mushrooms.

"Raine, you can tell me anything," I said. "The angels are going to look into this. They might ask you questions if they learn you fought with this guy just before he was killed."

She stared at me, her face paling. "What makes you think he was killed?"

"The huge head wound," I said. "He didn't slip and fall. Somebody did that to him."

She spun her empty glass on the bar. "What if I did see this guy before he died? That doesn't mean I had anything to do with his death."

"Hypothetically, let's say you did know him. What did you argue about?"

She blew out a breath. "It was nothing. I remember now, I hadn't been here long before this smooth-talking guy in a suit started coming on to me. He asked me out."

"Okay," I said. "And you didn't know him?"

"Never seen him before," Raine said. "He wouldn't take no for an answer. I turned him down, and he got mean. I decided to make sure he didn't try again."

I tilted my head. "But he knew your name. If you'd only just met, how come he knew who you were?"

"You don't know that." Her eyes narrowed.

"I do. The witness who saw you arguing said he yelled your name as you walked away."

"That means nothing. What if he did know my name? Maybe I told him. Maybe I thought he was cute and I might go out with him, but then he got too pushy."

She was lying. "I'm just trying to find out what happened to him. You need to have your story straight if the angels ask you questions."

"I don't need to have my story straight, since I'm not involved," Raine said. "Stop making a big deal out of this."

"It is a big deal if he was murdered and the angels are looking for who killed him."

She flattened her hands on the bar. "Apart from the head wound, which could have happened in loads of different ways, what evidence do you have to suggest he was murdered?"

I paused. "You don't get a wound like that from a simple trip. And there was no weapon in the store room."

"It's possible. You fall the wrong way and hit something hard. He could have become disoriented, crawled to Abigail's, and died there. It could be an accident."

"What about the snake? I think the killer used him as a kind of guard, so John couldn't get away. Maybe the snake cornered him, and the killer finished him off."

"Why not just use the snake to kill John?" Raine asked.

I rubbed my still sore arm. That was a valid point. Goliath could easily squeeze someone to death.

"You're making too much of this," she said. "I didn't know the guy. You don't even know he was killed. Why are you poking around in this?"

"Because your name's been mentioned," I said. "If John was murdered, I want to make sure you had nothing to do with it."

Her eyebrows shot up. "Tempest! You can't believe I'd kill someone?"

I sighed. I didn't think my cousin was a killer, but somehow, Raine was involved. She knew this guy. Something was going on here. Something Raine didn't want me to know about.

"Where were you last night?" I asked.

Her lips thinned. "You're checking my alibi? Don't you trust me?"

I did want to trust her, but she was hiding something. "I'm just asking what the angels will ask. Where were you last night? John died sometime last night."

"Then it wasn't me," Raine said. "I was with Azura."

"All night?"

"Pretty much. We did a joint shift at the cemetery then we headed back home and went to sleep."

Which meant, once Azura was asleep, Raine could have gone out on her own. She could have met John, confronted him, and things got out of hand.

"You're sure you don't know him?" I asked.

Raine stood slowly, fury sparkling in her eyes. "I didn't kill this guy." Her gaze shifted. "Azura! Get over here."

Azura hurried over with Wiggles. "You should see what Wiggles can do. He—"

"What were we doing last night?" Raine asked.

Azura's eyebrows rose. "Not much. We went to the cemetery for a few hours and hung out with the demons. Then we got something to eat and headed to Auntie Cora's. Why?"

"And then what?" Raine asked.

"We went to bed." She glanced from me to Raine. "What's going on?"

"Nothing's going on," I said. "We're just clearing something up."

"Tempest has a problem with me," Raine said.

I lifted a hand. "I don't have a problem with you." But something weird was going on, and it was something Raine was involved in, even though she wouldn't admit to it.

Azura's expression turned quizzical. "I don't get it. What are you two fighting about?"

"I'll tell you later." Raine grabbed her sister's arm. "Let's get out of here."

"We've only just arrived." Azura looked at the mushrooms on the bar. "I haven't even had a drink."

"We're not welcome." Raine dragged her away.

I sighed as I watched them go.

"Did you get anything useful?" Wiggles asked.

"Not much, other than the fact Raine's not being honest. She quizzed me just as hard as I did her. She knew John, but she wouldn't say how she knew him. She made up some excuse about him asking her out and him getting heavy when she turned him down."

"How do you think she knows him?" he asked.

"I don't know, but we need to find out before the angels do. Otherwise, they might decide Raine's a good suspect in this murder. We both know what happens when they do that."

"Innocent lives are ruined as they bumble around and make stuff up."

I snorted a laugh. "Pretty much."

"So, we're investigating this murder?"

"Only until Raine's in the clear." And that needed to happen fast. The angels might not be super smart, but they'd catch up, eventually. When they did, Raine would be in trouble.

Chapter 8

I was up early the next day. I had a quick shower, after cleaning the bath of Bandit's furry soap scum residue, dressed, and grabbed my keys.

"You two be good now," I said to Wiggles and Bandit.

"I'll keep an eye on her," Wiggles said.

"I don't need anybody to keep an eye on me," Bandit sneered. "And certainly not some foul-smelling hellhound. When was the last time you took a bath?"

"I bathe," Wiggles said. "This scent is an acquired taste. Certainly not one for your palate."

"Quite right. My nose is far too refined for your stench."

"The door's right there if you don't want to stay," Wiggles said.

"Quieten down," I said. "I won't be gone long. I need to see how the angels are progressing with their investigation and make sure they haven't decided to target Raine."

"I should come with you," Wiggles said.

"Stay here for now," I said. "I'll bring you back something nice."

"Doughnuts," Wiggles said.

"A ripe pineapple," Bandit said, "and maybe some cherries."

I shook my head. "I'll see what I can do. Stay here. Don't cause trouble. I'll be back soon." I headed down the stairs and out the door. The angels had had a whole day to investigate what happened to John. Hopefully, they'd made progress and that progress hadn't led them to my cousin.

I headed through the doors of Angel Force and over to the reception where Dominic stood.

He grinned at me. "I hope you're not here to report a crime. We're super busy at the moment, and several angels are on their holidays. Lucky things. I wish I was on holiday."

"Actually, I'm checking to see what happened with that guy found in Abigail's store. Any news?"

"We're still processing things," Dominic said. "Cassiel's looking at the body."

"It was definitely murder?"

He nodded. "It looks like it. Mr. Smith took a serious hit to the side of his head."

"Any evidence on the body?"

"There might be. Although, that snake messed things up. It partially crushed him."

I shuddered. "Before or after he died?"

"Possibly before," Dominic said. "Several ribs were broken. If the head wound didn't get him, the snake most certainly did."

"Any idea who used magic on the snake?" I asked.

"It vanished as soon as Abigail touched him," Dominic said. "Whatever residue of magic was there was wiped away. That's not going to lead us to the killer."

"Do you have any suspects in the frame?" I asked as casually as possible.

"We're asking around, but no one knows this guy. He hasn't been here long and wasn't renting a room at the hotel. We don't know where he was staying."

"Something will turn up." I smiled at Dominic. "You just have to keep asking questions."

The door behind him opened. Dazielle poked her head out and scowled when she spotted me.

I grimaced in response. "Morning."

"Let me guess. You can't stay away from this murder investigation." Dazielle walked over.

"I'm a concerned citizen," I said. "I did find the body, after all."

"Yes, thanks to your magic cat." Dazielle tilted her head. "Have you seen that cat since she fled the crime scene?"

"No idea where she is." Bandit was my secret weapon for now. "Have you got any suspects for John's murder yet?"

"Other than you?"

"Hey! I'm the innocent party here. I was at Cloven Hoof on the night of his murder and didn't get to bed until late. I've got plenty of witnesses if you need to corroborate that."

"I might just do that," Dazielle said.

Same old Dazielle, always trying to put me in the frame. "So, any idea who might have done this?"

Her gaze slid to Dominic. "I suspect you already know the answer if you've been here for long."

Dominic ducked his head and looked at some papers in front of him.

"I only want to make sure it's safe to walk our streets," I said.

"Of course, it's safe," Dazielle said. "We're still looking into who did this. The name John Smith isn't real, though. There's no record of him in our system, and we can't find anything from his fingerprints."

"He doesn't have a criminal record?"

"No, he doesn't have any fingerprints," she said.

My eyes widened. "How does that happen?"

"Because they've been burned off."

"Whoa! That's dodgy. Who would burn off their own fingerprints?" I asked.

"Someone who doesn't want to be identified," Dazielle said.

This murder was just getting weirder. Still, it was a relief they weren't mentioning Raine. Dazielle wouldn't resist prodding me if a member of my family was involved in this. But until they discovered what had happened, I'd keep doing my own discreet digging and find out exactly how Raine was involved.

"Is there anything more you'd like to tell us about the victim?" Dazielle asked.

"Nope. I know nothing about any of this," I said.

"Then you need to leave," Dazielle said.

"My thoughts exactly. Have a nice day." I turned and left Angel Force. Time was on my side for now. If the angels didn't even know who this elusive John Smith was, there was no way to identify him. He was a stranger in the village, and no one seemed to know anything about him. That gave me a chance to ask around and gather a fuller picture of what Raine was doing with him.

I headed over to Fur Baby Emporium. Abigail could have useful information now she'd gotten over her shock of discovering a body in her store room.

I headed into the store. There were a few people browsing, but it was early, so it wasn't busy. I raised my hand, and Abigail hurried over.

"How are you doing after yesterday?" I asked.

"Still in shock," she said. "I can't figure out what that poor man was doing in my store."

"It is weird," I said. "You definitely didn't know him?"

Abigail scooped up a sleek white cat that wandered past and started grooming her. "No, and I didn't want to get to know him. I don't like to speak ill of the dead, but after he let my toads out, I wasn't happy. It's such an impolite thing to do. The toads are still off their food. Toads are fragile."

I bit my bottom lip. I hadn't really thought about Abigail being involved with this, certainly not as the killer, but she had argued with this guy just before he'd died, and his body was found in her store. Maybe I'd overlooked the obvious killer.

"You don't remember ever seeing him here before?" I asked. "He could have come in when you were busy."

"No, he was a first-time visitor," Abigail said.

"Was he only interested in the toads?" I asked.

"He looked at lots of different familiars. Why do you ask?"

"You don't think he wanted something else from the store? He could have released those toads as a distraction," I said. "We were all occupied collecting them after he took them out of the glass case."

Her eyes widened. "Do you think he planned to rob me?"

"I didn't say robbery."

Her gaze whisked around the store.

"I know how valuable your familiars are. You haven't lost any since he came in, have you?"

Her eyes went even wider. "I haven't done a check today. I've been so flustered after the discovery of the body, and the angels were here for a long time yesterday. I was exhausted after they left. And I had all my new stock to unpack. Could he have stolen a familiar?" Her hand went to her mouth. "I'll need to check right away."

"I can help," I said. This was the perfect opportunity to keep quizzing Abigail and look around the store to see what the angels might have missed.

"That would be great! I've got a full list of familiars. Give me a second to grab it." Abigail hurried away and returned with five sheets of paper. "I've got three hundred and fifty familiars in stock."

"So many?"

"Many of them share cages. They like to be with friends. I can get through a check in half an hour if I'm quick. You start on the left side, and I'll start over here."

"Which side is Goliath on?" I asked.

She smiled and patted my arm. "Don't worry. I'll deal with him. And since that spell was removed, he's back to his normal sweet self. The poor guy must be in shock."

"I imagine so. I heard from the angels that he did some damage to John's body." I started counting owls.

Abigail shook her head. "It's a terrible business, but Goliath isn't a killer. He's a gentle giant. I let him sleep in my bed last night to make sure he didn't go into shock. That can kill a snake."

Abigail was either crazy brave or a little insane. Maybe that also came with a side order of killer instinct when it came to protecting her familiars.

I checked all the multi-colored canaries and the tawny owls before looking over at her. "Have you got any idea why John ended up in the back of your store?"

She finished counting her tortoises before shaking her head. "No idea. I made it clear he wasn't welcome to return. Although, I did let him out the door at the back after the incident with the toads, so he knew how to get in that way."

"Is anyone missing?"

"Not so far? How about you?"

"All present and correct so far." I started on the chameleons, who kept shifting around and changing color, making them difficult to count.

Abigail checked off numbers on several cages of rabbits. "I can't imagine what he'd want with my familiars. He had no respect for the toads."

"Maybe he just didn't like toads."

She hissed air through her teeth. "There must be something wrong with a person if they don't like toads or any creature for that matter. I'm just glad he didn't hurt any of them."

"And if he had?" I kept my tone neutral.

"We'd have had words."

Abigail was fiercely protective of her familiars. Could she have done something to John because she considered him a threat? Maybe she'd found him lurking outside the store and confronted him.

"You weren't around on the night of John's murder, were you?" I kept my attention on the brilliant gold parakeet in front of me, whose eyes sparkled, and tiny bubbles of magic drifted out of its mouth every time it chirped.

She glanced at me. "The angels said he was killed in the early hours of the morning."

Which wasn't an answer. "And where were you?"

"The angels have my alibi," she said.

"Which is..."

Her brows lowered. "I was home alone. I normally close the store around eight o'clock, and I was in bed by ten. I would have been asleep when John was killed."

Abigail lived alone, so that wasn't the best of alibis. Just like Raine, she could have snuck out and dealt with John without anyone seeing her. But how would she know he'd come back to her store? Maybe she'd seen him later in the day and asked him to come back. She might have held a grudge that he'd mistreated her familiars and planned to do something about it. She thought sleeping with a giant snake was normal behavior, so anything was possible.

"Do the angels have any idea who might have wanted to hurt John?" I asked.

Abigail ticked off more rabbits and moved on to the cats. She looked around the store before walking over. "I don't like to gossip, but when he was in the store that day, he was attracting attention from Trixie."

"He was?" I lowered my list of familiars. "She's with Mannie. I thought they were happy."

"That's not for me to say. John was here for a good hour, and a lot of the time, Trixie was flirting with him. She was practically glued to his side."

"Maybe she was just helping him decide on a familiar."

"Trixie's amazing with the animals but not so great with the customers. I sometimes think things get lost in translation, but she can be overly familiar. And she was certainly that with John. She kept touching his arm and doing that annoying fluttering with her false eyelashes."

"How did John handle this flirting?"

"He was enjoying himself. It wasn't until I told Trixie to get on with her work that she left him alone. That was just before you came into the store with your sister. It wasn't long after that John started misbehaving."

"You don't think Trixie has anything to do with what happened to John?" I asked.

Abigail shrugged. "I think it's unlikely, but she has a temper. She gets passionate about certain things, and I imagine being with Mannie must wear your patience. He's a tricky dwarf to deal with, and there's that big age gap between them. It must wear her down being with him. I almost don't blame her for looking for another option. Although, not when I'm paying her to work in the store."

Trixie and John? Could she know him? Maybe she was flirting with John and he turned her down, or they went out that night and something went wrong.

"Is Trixie working today?" I asked.

"No, she only does three days a week. I'm glad she's not here today. She doesn't handle stress well. I haven't told her what happened in the store room yet. I want to keep it as quiet as possible. It won't do the business's reputation any good if people learn about someone being killed here." Abigail tilted her chin. "I trust you're being discreet, Tempest."

"Of course. It's not my business."

"And I appreciate you not talking about it," Abigail said. "The sooner this matter is cleared up, the better. I'm sure this John simply got on the wrong side of somebody and they fought. He must've come into the store and died here. It's just unfortunate luck."

Although that could be true, it still left out a big part of the puzzle. What about Goliath and the spell that had been put on him?

I tucked away that thought, along with the fact Abigail's alibi was anything but perfect.

We finished checking the familiars, and they were all accounted for. That ruled out the possibility that John had come back to steal valuable stock. It also made it less likely Abigail had killed him when she caught him doing something he shouldn't.

I handed the list back to her. "At least you don't need to worry that John stole from you. That would have been a great motive for you wanting him out of the way if you'd caught him taking your familiars."

Her laugh was startled. "Indeed, it would. I can assure you I had nothing to do with this horrible incident."

"Of course. The angels will figure this out." It was time for me to get out of here. I wanted to pay Trixie a visit, but before I did, I wanted to check in with Bandit.

She'd been in the store before I'd arrived with Aurora. She'd have seen Trixie and John flirting. She might even have overheard their conversation.

I said goodbye to Abigail and hurried out of the store back to Cloven Hoof.

As I reached the top of the stairs, there was a crash.

I hurried to get the door unlocked. I pushed it open wide, and my jaw dropped. I'd been burgled.

Chapter 9

I took a tentative step into my apartment. Chairs were overturned, the contents of most of the drawers had been tossed to the floor, and the food from the fridge lay scattered around.

The wooden fruit bowl from the kitchen counter tipped from side to side on the floor. That must have been the noise I heard when I was outside.

"Wiggles?" I looked around. There was no sign of him.

If the place had been broken into, what had happened to him? And where was Bandit? Why hadn't they stopped whoever had done this?

Wiggles' bed was flipped upside down, and there was a large slash across the back of it, the filling floating around on the floor as I walked past.

I looked into my bedroom. The covers were yanked off the bed and the pillows slung about. What did they want from my apartment? If it was a burglar hunting for the takings from Cloven Hoof, they were looking in the wrong place. The safe was downstairs and guarded with magic. Anyone foolish enough to try to get their hands on my profits would soon regret it.

I paused beside the smashed snow globe. My means of contacting Angel Force and letting them know I'd been burgled was gone. I had another one downstairs, so I could still report the crime. Nobody broke into my apartment and got away with it.

Scowling, I stamped down the stairs, certain that whoever it was, was long gone. They'd better be. If I caught them, I'd rip their head off.

I headed through the bar and skidded to a halt. Thudding came from the kitchen. The intruder must still be here.

I grabbed a heavy glass bottle from the shelf and tiptoed toward the entrance to the kitchen. I paused by the door as something smashed to the ground.

With gritted teeth, I slid the door open and peered inside.

Bandit sat on top of the kitchen counter, her paws resting on the edge of a large metal bowl.

I pushed the door open wider, the bottle still raised in my hand. "Where's the intruder?" I whispered.

Her ears flicked as she chewed on a grape. "What intruder?"

"Whoever trashed my apartment," I said. "Are they still here? Did you get a look at them?" I jumped as something thudded against the freezer door.

My brow wrinkled. That noise came from inside the freezer.

"There's no intruder," Bandit said. "Do you want some watermelon?"

"No, I don't want any watermelon." I lowered the bottle and placed it on the counter. "If there was no intruder, then what happened up there?"

"Your hellhound got stroppy," Bandit said.

My eyes widened, and my anger rose. "You're telling me that you and Wiggles made that mess?"

"He brought it on himself," she said. "He hid all the fruit. He told me I wouldn't get fed unless I found it for myself. He said it was a game. Who's laughing now?"

"You turned the place upside down in the hunt for a banana?"

Bandit scooped another grape out of the bowl with a paw and flipped it into her mouth before nodding.

"It's a wreck," I said.

"Wiggles is good at hiding things," Bandit said.

My eyes narrowed. "Where is he?"

There was another thump from the freezer. My gaze darted from Bandit back to the closed door. "You locked him in the deep freeze?"

Her pink tongue shot out as she licked fruit juice from her whiskers. "He's not the brightest of hounds. He most likely got himself stuck in there looking for steak."

"Then you should have let him out." I hurried to the door.

"Maybe he wants to be in there," she said.

I glared at Bandit as I yanked the door open.

Wiggles rolled out and lay on the floor on his back, blinking up at me. "I have no feeling in my paws."

"How long have you been in there?" I knelt and brushed ice off his fur.

"That evil cat tricked me," he said. "She told me there were steaks on the bottom shelf. She said she knew how to cook them. All I had to do was go in and get them."

"And you believed her?" I rubbed feeling back into his paws before rolling him onto his belly. The inside of the freezer door was covered in singe marks where he must have tried to burn his way out.

"I'd do anything for a juicy steak," Wiggles muttered.

Bandit snorted a laugh. "Told you. Not the brightest hellhound."

I snarled at her. "We're coming up with ground rules if you're staying with us."

"Where is that manky cat?" Wiggles staggered to his feet, a growl rumbling in his chest. "I'm going to turn her into a fur coat."

"You need to lose a little weight before I fit you," Bandit said.

Wiggles' red-eyed gaze shot to the counter. "Wait 'til you get down from there."

"No! No more fighting," I said. "This ends now. Bandit, don't lock Wiggles in any more rooms, especially not ones with sub-zero temperatures."

"I didn't do it," she said. "He wandered in, and the door clicked shut. How am I supposed to open a freezer door with paws like this? No opposable thumbs, you see. Now, when cats evolve thumbs, we'll conquer the world."

"You told me there were steaks," Wiggles said.

"Anyone can make a mistake," Bandit said.

"I don't care what happened," I said. "No more fighting. No more tricking Wiggles. And Wiggles, no more hiding Bandit's food."

"This isn't my fault," he said.

"And you two are cleaning up the apartment," I said. "The place is a mess."

"That was her fault," Wiggles said.

"I had nothing to do with that," Bandit said.

I shook my head. That cat had really gotten one over on Wiggles. There was a sneaky magic user inside this kitty cat. I'd need to watch my step around her, unless I wanted my underwear shredded and hairballs appearing in my shoes.

I blew out a breath. "While you were both wrecking my apartment, I was hunting for a killer."

"What did you find?" Wiggles glared at Bandit.

"I have a question about Trixie. Bandit, were you in the store when she was talking to John?" I asked.

Bandit nodded. "Sure. I was there all morning."

"And how was she acting around him?"

She tilted her head. "Sort of annoying, like she usually is. Trixie gets high-pitched when she's excited. It makes my ears hurt."

"Did they flirt with each other?" I asked.

"Oh! Sure. She was all over him like a cheap suit."

That confirmed what Abigail told me. "And what about Abigail? Did she seem to know John?"

Her ears twitched. "I'm pretty sure they didn't know each other."

"You don't think we should consider her as a suspect?"

"Hey! Since when has the cat been your sleuthing sidekick?" Wiggles bumped my leg with his head.

"She's not. But she was there."

"I have my uses, hound," Bandit said.

"Name one," he said.

I shook my head. "No bickering. Go on. You think Abigail's innocent."

"Not necessarily. I didn't say I trusted her," she said. "She's up to something that requires late night trips. She keeps sneaking out of the village. I followed her a couple of times."

"Does that include on the night of John's murder?" I asked.

Bandit nodded. "She left the store about eight o'clock but came back later. She had boxes with her. I'd managed to sneak back in and was hiding under one of the cages. She dropped off the boxes and disappeared. I followed her, and she went to the edge of the magic barrier and passed right through. About half an hour later, she came back with a load more boxes."

"What was in the boxes?" I asked.

"I didn't see," Bandit said.

I scrubbed my chin. "Did these late-night expeditions have anything to do with John? Did he catch Abigail doing something she shouldn't and confronted her?"

"I didn't see the guy around at that time," Bandit said. "Abigail went out, got the boxes, and put them on the counter. I went for a walk, and when I got back to the store, I found the body."

"That means Abigail lied about her alibi," I said. "She said she was asleep at the time of the murder."

"What did the angels have to say?" Wiggles hadn't stopped glaring at Bandit the whole time we'd been talking.

"They don't have any suspects, which is a good thing. But we need to speak to Trixie." I glanced at Wiggles. His expression held the threat of murder. "And this time, I'm not leaving the two of you alone."

"I'm not walking with her," Wiggles said. "I have a reputation in this village. I can't be seem looking remotely friendly with that thing."

"And I'm not spending any time near that stinky hound," Bandit shot back.

"You're both coming with me," I said. "I don't trust you on your own."

Wiggles grumbled, and Bandit growled.

"How about I keep you both separate? Wiggles, you can walk as normal. Bandit, I'll find a purse to put you in."

The cat's nose wrinkled. "You're going to carry me? Like you're my slave?"

"No! Not like I'm your slave. You're not staying in the apartment on your own until you've earned back my trust."

"Hah!" Wiggles barked out a laugh. "Tempest sees right through you."

I turned toward him. "Don't think you're in the clear. You'd better make sure you find all that fruit you've hidden. I don't want to discover a moldy banana under a couch cushion in three months. If I do, it'll be squished up and added to your food."

Wiggles' nose twitched. "I'll get it all out."

"Can I trust you both on your own if I go grab a purse?" I asked.

They eyeballed each other before nodding.

I raced upstairs, grabbed the biggest purse I could find, and hurried back down. It looked as if a few grapes had been thrown at Wiggles from Bandit's vantage point, but other than that, the kitchen was intact.

I placed the purse down and opened it. "Get in."

Bandit thoroughly examined the purse before nodding. "It's an acceptable mode of transport. I can stick my head out and see what's going on."

"But keep quiet," I said. "People are used to Wiggles speaking, but having another talking animal in the village will be a surprise."

"Where are we going?" Wiggles asked as Bandit took a moment to position herself in the purse.

"Mannie's house," I said. "It's Trixie's day off, so she's most likely there. I want to find out how much she knows about John and just how friendly they were."

"I should put on my bow tie if we're going to see the mayor," Wiggles said.

"You'll need more than a bow tie if you want to make a good impression," Bandit said.

"We don't have time for that," I said. "Let's move it. We have a killer to find."

We left Cloven Hoof and headed to the edge of the village. Mannie lived in a huge earth house that was partially submerged in the ground and came with a grass roof and a large chimney stack.

I hit the doorbell, and there was a booming ring inside the house.

A moment later, the door was opened by Trixie, dressed in a skin tight white dress.

"Tempest! And your little doggy." She leaned down and petted Wiggles' head. "Mannie's not here."

"Actually, I'm looking for you," I said. "Have you got a few minutes?"

"Of course. Can be my guest. You are welcome." She stepped back and gestured us inside.

The hallway was cluttered with large oil paintings of what looked like members of Mannie's family. They were all stout dwarves with luxurious beards. Despite the sun columns providing a sprinkling of light, it was gloomy in the hallway.

"This way. You have tea?" Trixie asked.

"Tea would be good. Thanks." I walked behind her, gently easing Bandit's head back into the purse as she peered around.

I followed Trixie into a lounge, where heavy red velvet drapes hung at the small windows, making it even gloomier.

"Sit. I get tea and baklava. The very best." Trixie nodded before hurrying out of the room.

"It's the first time I've been in here," Wiggles said. "Mannie sure likes his velvet." He sniffed the green velvet couch I sat on as I looked around.

There was a display of dwarf battle hammers on one wall, and more oil paintings of dwarves looked down at us. Mannie was proud of his history.

Trixie returned a moment later, a silver tray in her hands. There was a large Russian tea urn and a plate of sweet pastries resting on it.

She smiled at me. "I'm a lucky girl, no? Mannie get me the best things."

"You're living here now?" I asked.

"Oh, yes. He moved me in fast. He knows his mind. He's a confident dwarf."

I bit my bottom lip. "He is that. It's good you're getting on so well."

"He make me happy. Tea?" Trixie asked.

"Looks good. Thanks." The tea that came out was almost black and smelt of lemon and cinnamon.

"Hope you like it strong." She passed me a cup.

I took a sip, and my eyebrows shot up.

She giggled. "Make you proper Russian tea with sugar and citrus, plus cinnamon sticks and cloves. You like?"

I took another sip. It was pretty good. "I do."

"From my hometown. Mannie imports." Trixie settled in a seat and pointed at Wiggles, whose gaze was fixed on the glazed pastries. "Your puppy eats baklava?"

"He shouldn't but maybe one piece," I said.

Trixie placed a piece on a plate and put it on the ground. She laughed as he gobbled it in one bite. "Greedy puppy."

"What about me?" Bandit whispered.

I pressed the top of the purse shut.

"Did you say something?" Trixie asked.

"No, nothing. Just appreciating the tea and baklava," I said.

She nodded. "I have more. Mannie spoils me."

"Banana?" Bandit whispered way too loudly.

Trixie tilted her head, her expression puzzled.

"So, you're enjoying your job at Fur Baby Emporium?" I asked.

"Very much. Nice place. Love the animals. Mannie got me the job. I enjoy it. I like Abigail. She good to me."

"Do you remember—"

"Oh! You have a cat in your bag." Trixie pointed at my purse.

I scowled and looked down at Bandit's head. "She's not my cat. But yes, she came along for the ride. Getting back to Fur—"

"Wait!" Trixie jabbed a finger at Bandit. "From our store. You have our cat."

"No, I mean, technically, I'm looking after her but not forever."

"You adopted her?" Trixie's eyes narrowed. "You did not pay for her."

I grimaced. "No, I didn't, but I've definitely not adopted her. Bandit's on an extended loan."

"You pay money for that cat. Very special cat," Trixie said. "You give me money now. I earn commission on each sale."

I raised a hand. "No! I'm not buying the cat."

She scowled. "You have stolen from store?"

"Absolutely not. This is a short-term deal. I'll return Bandit to the store as soon as possible," I said. "I'm not looking to make a purchase."

Bandit growled and swiped a paw at me.

"You name her?" Trixie asked.

I gritted my teeth. "Bandit suited her wily nature. So, getting back to the store. Have the angels been in touch about what's been going on?"

She sighed and nodded as she topped up her cup, her gaze still on Bandit. "The man dead in the back."

"Yes, they think it was murder."

Trixie shook her head. "So sad."

"Did you know him?" I asked.

"Only from the store."

"Was that the first time you'd met him?"

"Yes. He said he was new to village. Looking for a familiar."

"Did you believe him?"

"Of course. Why come to Emporium if you don't want familiar?"

"He was a good-looking guy, don't you think?"

She pursed her lips. "Not unattractive."

"Was he nice to you?"

Trixie popped a piece of sticky baklava in her mouth and chewed. "He was polite. A gentleman."

"Did you like him?"

Her eyebrows rose. "I guess so."

"You were flirting with him." Bandit's head appeared out of the purse again.

Trixie's jaw dropped, and she dropped her baklava. "She talks?"

"She does." I wished I hadn't brought Bandit with me, but I valued the contents of my apartment too much to leave her on her own.

"Then she worth a lot more money." Trixie snapped her fingers at me. "You pay now."

"No, you can have her back," I said.

"I'm going nowhere." Bandit glared at me. "I saw you, Trixie. You were flirting with that guy. You kept fluttering your lashes and touching his arm."

"No! Not flirting. Friendly. Be nice to customers, Abigail says. Make them buy." Trixie shrugged. "I told to flirt. I do my job."

"And they buy something when you flirt with them?" I asked.

"All the time." She looked away.

"The angels will want to know everything," I said. "You need to get your story straight. Did you see John Smith outside the store after you got to know him that day?"

She sighed. "I want no trouble."

"Then tell the truth."

Her mouth sagged. "I tell you. I do nothing bad. We met and talked. He was charming."

"Did anything happen?" I asked.

She looked around the room. "A simple kiss. It meant nothing. As soon as it happened, I regret it."

The front door opened and banged shut. "I'm home, Princess."

Trixie jumped to her feet, her cheeks paling. "Say nothing to Mannie. He must never know. He has temper. He kill me."

I glanced over my shoulder. "What did you do after you kissed John?"

Trixie flapped her hands in the air. "Nothing. Come home. I was with my Mannie. I did not see John anymore."

"You didn't meet up later that night?" I asked.

"Shush!" Her panicked gaze went to the door. "No. Please, no tell Mannie. It is for best if you stay quiet. You understand?"

Mannie strolled through the door. He stopped when he saw me. "Tempest! This is a nice surprise. You're keeping Trixie company?"

I glanced at her. Terror was written across her face. "I am. We dropped by for a catch up. I expect you've heard what happened at the store."

Mannie nodded. He walked over and kissed Trixie. "Such a shock for you, my sweetie. How are you managing, my love?"

Trixie wrapped her arms around him and shot me a grateful look. "Is stressful."

"There, there, of course it is." He patted her back. "Perhaps you shouldn't work there anymore."

She pulled back. "No! Love my job."

"The angels think it was murder," I said.

Mannie shook his head. "It's a mystery; that's what it is. No one knows who this man was or why he was in the village."

"That's just what I was asking Trixie," I said. "If she'd seen him before or if he'd told her what he was doing in Willow Tree Falls."

"I said no," Trixie said swiftly. "Never seen him before. Don't know him."

"Of course, you don't." Mannie patted her hand as they sat on the couch together.

"Barely remember him," Trixie said. "Always so busy."

"You can't be expected to remember every customer who comes into the store," Mannie said.

"You didn't see John around the store when you left that evening?" I asked Trixie.

"Already said no," she replied sharply. "Not interested in him. Come home. Prepare meal for my man. Make him comfortable."

Mannie chuckled. "We had rather a lot to drink that evening. You kept topping up my beer mug. I was quite merry by the end of the night. I don't even remember how I got to bed."

My eyes narrowed. Had Trixie deliberately gotten Mannie drunk? Did she want him passed out, so she could slip out and meet John?

"You deserved it," Trixie said. "Work too hard."

"I do it all for you," Mannie said. "And the museum has really taken off. It's very popular. Tempest, have you been there recently?"

The village had opened a museum of magic and witchcraft a few months ago. The opening event had been spectacular for all the wrong reasons when the body of a witch was found on the ducking stool.

"Not recently," I said.

"We have new exhibits. You'd enjoy them," he said.

"I'll make sure to drop by." I grabbed two baklavas and ate them as I discreetly studied Trixie. She was jumpy, but I couldn't decide if she was worried about being caught cheating, or if it was because she was hiding exactly what happened that night with John. "Well, I should get going. I don't want to disturb the rest of your day."

"Very good," Mannie said. "Trixie, show them out."

She nodded and followed me and Wiggles. She caught hold of my arm as I walked to the front door.

"Please, keep quiet. I make mistake. I had nothing to do with man's death."

"And you're sure you've never met him before?" I asked. "You don't know why he was in Willow Tree Falls?"

She shook her head. "I know nothing. I got tempted. Mannie's a good man, but he is..." she gestured over her shoulder. "He can be difficult. He works a lot. I get lonely. I meant no harm."

I bit my bottom lip. Mannie was a pompous, officious dwarf. Trixie must have the patience of a saint to live with him.

"Have the cat for free," she said. "You say nothing about my involvement, and I forget I see her. Deal?"

I looked at Bandit. "No deal. I'm not keeping her."

Her grip tightened on my arm. "Please, don't say anything."

I blew out a breath. "I'll keep quiet for now."

"Good, good," Trixie said. "If you need anything from store, just say. I get you for free. Keep this between us. I didn't kill that man. Like my life as is. I got my head turned by handsome face. No crime in that, is there?"

There could be, if that handsome face rejected her, and she'd done something about it.

We said our goodbyes, and I left the house.

"What do you think?" Wiggles asked.

"She's a good suspect," I said.

"She has a motive and a lousy alibi," Bandit said. "She was obviously into the dead guy. I reckon they met up late that night and things got hot and heavy. Either he turned her down, or she did to him when he wanted to take things too far, and it got out of hand."

"Trixie also has a bad alibi," Wiggles said.

I nodded. "No alibi. She got Mannie drunk that night. He might believe they'd been together all night, but if he was passed out drunk, Trixie would have been free to come and go as she liked, and he'd never know what was going on. Mannie can't vouch for Trixie's whereabouts on the night of the murder."

"And she'd have access to the store," Bandit said. "It's the perfect place for her to have a secret liaison with her lover."

"I was about to say that," Wiggles said. "What's the next move?"

"I'm not sure," I said. "But Trixie's a much better suspect than Raine. It looks like my cousin could be in the clear."

Chapter 10

"You'll have to throw out that cushion." I lounged on the couch as Bandit and Wiggles finished clearing up the apartment. It was their punishment for trashing it in the first place.

"I need a new bed." Wiggles looked mournfully at his former lounge bed. "That monster shredded mine."

"You shouldn't have hidden a grape inside it," Bandit said. "I could smell it, but I couldn't see it. It's your own fault."

"You didn't need to use your claws," Wiggles said. "If you'd nudged it aside with your foot, instead of slashing at it like you were an extra in a horror movie, you'd have spotted the grape straight away."

"I don't care who did what," I said as Wiggles tugged the rug back into position with his teeth. "It doesn't happen again. If any of this gets moved out of place, you're both going to need to find new homes."

Wiggles spat out the rug and stared at me. "You can't throw me out because of her bad behavior. None of this would have happened if it wasn't for that spiteful furball."

"Who hid the fruit?" Bandit asked.

"It doesn't matter," I growled out. "Now, finish up, then we'll go see Aurora."

Wiggles bounced on his paws. "She always has the best cookies."

"Does she do fruit?" Bandit asked. "I could go for a big bowl of oranges right about now. All this redecorating works up an appetite."

I stood and pulled on my boots as they finished up. I'd been checking in on Aurora most days since she reopened the store. She put on a brave face, but when she thought nobody was looking, hurt shone in her eyes. I wanted to be around to make sure that sad look didn't last for long.

I did a quick look around the apartment and nodded. There were a few things beyond repair, but the place was back to its normal, reasonably tidy state.

Bandit hopped back in her carry purse, and the three of us left the club and headed over to Heaven's Door.

I pushed open the door and saw several customers browsing the shelves. I knew it wouldn't be long before word got out that Aurora's store was open for business again. She was always popular. She had a great way with customers and would always help someone if they had problems with a spell or needed assistance with a health niggle.

Aurora lifted a hand and smiled. "How's everything going?"

"Busy day so far," I said.

"Any word on what's been going on at Abigail's?" She petted Wiggles' head as he bounced in front of her, greedy for attention.

"That's what's been keeping me busy," I said.

"Time for tea and brownies?" she asked.

I grinned. "Always."

Her gaze drifted to my purse. "Oh! That's the cat from Abigail's store. What's she doing with you?"

"Long story." I gave her the key points as to Bandit's arrival, including her ability to talk and the chaos she'd caused since she moved in.

Aurora laughed as she tickled Bandit's head. "She's a cutie and really pretty now she's had a bath."

Bandit purred and rubbed against Aurora's hand.

"Weirdly, she also loves fruit. If you've got any spare, she'd appreciate it," I said.

"Bananas," Bandit said, "or oranges. Anything, really."

"Okay, fruit! I'll see what I can do." Aurora hurried away.

"You two be on your best behavior," I said. "Aurora doesn't need to handle your nonsense. She's a bit fragile."

"Aurora loves me," Wiggles said. "She knows I'd never cause trouble."

"Then she doesn't know you very well," Bandit said.

"Hush." I glanced around the store again. The shelves weren't full yet, and the book stack looked out of order. Aurora had really let the place go when she'd been distracted by Toby, but things were getting back to normal.

She strolled in through the back room and passed around brownies, tea, and a small bowl of chopped up apples and oranges for Bandit.

Bandit hopped out of my purse and licked her lips before purring and rubbing around Aurora again.

"She's a changed cat," Aurora said. "What an angel."

"Don't be fooled," Wiggles said. "Pure evil runs through that cat's veins."

Bandit turned and hissed at Wiggles before digging into her fruit.

Aurora glanced at me, and her eyebrows rose.

"They have a tricky relationship," I said.

She sipped her tea. "So, what have you heard about this murder?"

I leaned closer. "So far, there are three people who could be involved." I gave her a quick update about Abigail's dubious night-time activities, Trixie's secret liaison with the victim, and Raine's false alibi.

When I mentioned our cousin, Aurora choked on her tea. "I can't believe she'd be involved."

"Neither could I until I talked to her at the club," I said. "Raine's being weird."

"What makes you say that?"

"She was seen talking to the victim the day he died," I said.

"Who saw her?" Aurora asked.

"I did," Bandit said.

She grinned. "I still can't believe you have a talking hellhound and a talking cat. Well, a magical being transformed into a cat."

"It shocked the fur off me as well," Bandit said. "Growing a tail takes a bit of getting used to."

"Anyway, getting back to the murder, Bandit saw John and Raine arguing," I said. "Raine made out he'd been coming onto her and asked her out, but she turned him down."

"And this John guy didn't like taking no for an answer?" Aurora asked.

"That's what she reckons, but she was hiding something, and I'm pretty sure she got Azura to cover for her and give her an alibi for that night. Why would she do that if she's not involved?"

"Could it be something to do with her new job?" Aurora asked.

I tilted my head. "What new job?"

"I don't know much about it, but Granny Dottie mentioned it. It's something official. She started talking and got all flustered as if she realized she shouldn't be telling anybody what she knew."

"What kind of job would Raine have that needs to be kept a secret?" I asked.

"Hey! You did that deliberately." Wiggles glared up at Bandit, who smiled smugly down at him.

"Tempest! Bandit swiped a pen off the counter, and it hit me on the head," Wiggles said.

Bandit raised a paw. "I'm a cat. It's in my nature. You can't fight it. We enjoy knocking things to the ground."

"Stop messing around, you two," I said. "Remember, best behavior while we're here."

"I'm being on my best catlike behavior," Bandit said. "I can't help it that I have these urges. Ever since I was turned into this adorable furry form,

I get these weird desires to shred things with my claws and knock things off tables. And don't get me started on when I see a bird in a tree. It's like my kryptonite. I can't keep away. The bird might be at the top of the tree, and I have no chance of getting it, but I have to chatter at it like a crazy... well, crazy cat."

I gestured at her to stop talking. "Okay, so you're a cat, which makes you a little... temperamental. But less throwing things on Wiggles' head."

"As a hellhound, I often have a desire to spout flames at people I don't like." Wiggles backed up a few steps. "Does that mean I can give in to my natural urges?"

"No, you don't. No flames in Aurora's store," I said.

Wiggles cleared his throat. "I can't help it. I'm just like that evil creature you're letting sit on the countertop. I have to do it."

"No!" I recognized the determined glint in his red eyes. "No fire."

"But you never let me sit on the countertop. It's making me angry. When I get angry, I blast flames." Smoke billowed from his nose.

"Wiggles, I'd let you sit on the countertop if you were a bit smaller," Aurora said. "But you're such a chunky little guy. It would be a squeeze to fit you, my new herbal promotion, and the register. Where would the customers put their goods?"

"Hah! She just called you fat," Bandit said.

Aurora glanced at me. "No. You're definitely not fat. You just fill out your muscles nicely. It's better that you have a few extra pounds on you. It makes you nice and squishy when I hug you."

"That means you're fat," Bandit said.

"That's it! You're getting flamed," Wiggles said.

Aurora strode out from behind the counter and grabbed Wiggles around the belly, flipping him over her shoulder. "No, you don't. Both of you need to go on the naughty step."

"The naughty what?" I asked.

"That's what all badly behaving children need." She carried Wiggles to the scratchy rug by the entrance door to the store. "Wiggles, you sit there and think about what you were about to do and if it was appropriate."

He blinked up at her, shock on his face. "What about the furball on your counter?"

Aurora strode over, scooped Bandit into her arms and set her on the scratchy rug. "Both of you sit there and behave. If you're going to live with Tempest, you must learn to get along together."

Bandit placed a foot off the rug.

Aurora stunned me by conjuring a threatening rain cloud and hovering it over Bandit's head. "Stay on the naughty rug."

"Is it the rug who's naughty or us?" Bandit eyed the cloud.

Aurora arched a brow. "Don't be clever with me. You both sit and have a think. No more squabbling, or it's the last time you get fruit and cookies from me."

Bandit shuffled her butt a few times.

Wiggles grabbed her tail in his teeth. "Don't move. Aurora makes great cookies. I'm not missing out because of you."

She hissed at him but finally settled on the rug. "Fine. I'm sitting like the embarrassingly good kitty you've mistaken me for."

Aurora turned to me and winked before walking behind the counter.

"You're a natural with them," I said. "Maybe it is time you got a few pets around here. Starting with a familiar. Have you given it anymore thought?"

She tilted her head from side to side. "I'm still thinking about something cute. I'm not sure, though. It might be too soon to make such a commitment."

"It's just what you need," I said. "Why don't we—"

Bandit screeched and leaped onto Wiggles' back as the store door was flung open.

"Get off me! Tempest, this cat has to go." Wiggles bucked until Bandit bounced off and landed on a shelf with a dignified grace.

Rhett Blackthorn stood in the doorway, his expression concerned. "Have you seen who's in the village?"

"Hello to you, too," I said. "What's going on?"

"I've just seen someone from the Magic Council roll up and meet with the angels." He strode over, kissed me, and nodded a greeting at Aurora.

"What's the Magic Council doing here?" Aurora asked.

"Whenever they're in the village, it's never good news. It's not trouble for the gang, is it?" I asked Rhett.

"Why would they be interested in us?" He quirked an eyebrow. "We're the good guys."

I grinned. Rhett and the angels weren't friends, and his occasional slip over to the wrong side of magical law meant he got noticed by the higher up powers, including the Magic Council.

"Did you see who it is?" Aurora asked.

He nodded. "Viggo Blowhard. He's a specialist in hunting down dark magic users."

My stomach flipped. "We'd better take a look." I scooped Bandit from the shelf, placed her in the purse, and gestured for Wiggles to follow.

"New pet?" Rhett asked as he watched me tuck Bandit away.

"Not as such. I'll see you later, Aurora." I lifted a hand as we hurried out the store. "I'll explain on the way. Let's see what the Magic Council wants with Willow Tree Falls."

Chapter 11

We'd been lurking around Angel Force for ten minutes, waiting for any sign of Viggo. In that time, I'd caught Rhett up on the murder at Abigail's and my new temporary family member, Bandit.

We were tucked out of the way, close to some trees, so we wouldn't be spotted by the angels as we waited to see what was happening.

"How do you know Viggo?" I asked Rhett.

"We've had dealings," he said. "He got hold of bad information on the gang a few years ago. He spent a month hassling us and trying to get somebody to talk. It didn't work. My gang's loyal to me. That didn't stop him from using underhanded tactics to try to get what he wanted. I don't trust the guy."

Rhett didn't trust many people, but that didn't mean his instincts weren't right when it came to the Magic Council.

"This visit might have something to do with the murder in Abigail's store." I set down my purse to let Bandit out.

"From what you've told me, it sounds more like a crime of passion than anything to do with the Magic Council," Rhett said.

"It's a bit of a coincidence that they send someone here so soon after the murder." I grabbed Rhett's arm as the door to Angel Force opened.

Dazielle walked out, closely followed by a short, squat guy wearing a gray suit.

"That's Viggo," Rhett muttered.

I studied him as Viggo talked to Dazielle. He stood with his legs wide apart and his hands behind his back, oozing self-assurance. He shook hands with Dazielle and walked away, while she returned inside.

"We should grab him now while we have the chance," I said. "Find out what he's doing here."

Before Rhett had a chance to stop me, I stepped out from behind the tree and moved into Viggo's path.

He slowed, his dark gaze running over me slowly. "And you are?"

"Tempest Crypt. What are you doing in Willow Tree Falls?"

"One of the Crypt witches." He nodded. "I hear a lot about your family. Have you got your demon prison under control?"

"As always," I said. "Are you here about the murder?"

He lifted his chin, his expression cold. "That's not what I heard. It wasn't so long ago that we were thinking of replacing your family as prison guardians with a more capable set of witches."

My eyes narrowed. "We're very capable when it comes to keeping the prison secure. We've been looking after that prison for centuries. So, are you here about the murder?"

A sneer crossed his face. "Sometimes, things need to change. Powers wane and abilities are no longer suitable for the task in hand. We even considered forming a committee to discuss a suitable replacement. Find a family who caused a little less... drama."

My fingers flexed. He was trying to get a rise out of me. "Is that a no to you being in the village to deal with John Smith's murder?"

He chuckled. "I, however, voted against the idea of having the Crypt witches replaced. I've reviewed your family's history, and I have a certain amount of respect for what you do." Viggo's head tilted. "And I believe you're the witch who looks after her very own demon. That must keep you busy."

"I have an excellent planner that keeps me on time for everything. I never miss an appointment. How did you know John Smith?" I asked.

"I've even met your grandma a few times. How is she?" Viggo asked.

"Granny Dottie's in excellent health." I sighed. We could probably continue this question avoidance session for hours. "My demon's also thriving, but he's having trouble behaving himself. Usually, when I get angry with someone, so does he."

"Fascinating. And are you angry now?"

"Getting there."

His sneer only widened. "I suggested to the Magic Council we bring you in for questioning. You were having problems not so long ago, weren't you?"

"Nope. Everything's under control. Nothing to worry about here." I patted my chest. "How about the Magic Council? Everything peachy there?"

He bared his teeth. "It's a unique ability you have, being able to contain a demon while maintaining a degree of civility. Would you be open to a few simple tests? Purely for academic research purposes."

"No. What do you know about John Smith?"

Viggo's gaze went over my shoulder, and a scowl appeared on his face. "We have unwelcome company."

I sensed Rhett as a wave of tension slid over me. "He's always welcome."

Viggo's eyebrows rose a fraction. "Ah, I see. Darkness attracts. You're together?"

"What if we are?" I asked.

"You need to be more careful with the company you keep," Viggo said.

"I keep excellent company," I said.

"The evidence suggests otherwise," Viggo said. "Keeping out of trouble, Rhett?"

"As always." Rhett moved to my side. "Why are you here?"

Viggo shrugged. "Tempest is correct. I'm investigating this murder."

"How did you know the victim?" I asked. "Is John Smith even his real name?"

Viggo smirked. "It's a name he's used in the past."

"The murder must have a dark magic connection if you're here," Rhett said.

"You know me well," Viggo said.

"Why keep this a secret?" I asked. "Maybe we can help."

"Doubtful, but it's no secret." He crossed his arms over his chest. "There is a suggestion dark magic was involved, and I had plans to visit you, Tempest, and find out what you knew."

Rhett moved in front of me. "She has nothing to do with this."

I stepped to the side and touched his arm. "It's fine. I did find the body."

"And what did you sense when you found... John?" Viggo asked.

I glanced at Rhett. "The spell used on the snake was dark. Abigail touched the snake and transferred the magic to her. I felt it. It was nothing like the original power of the spell, but there were remnants of dark energy."

Viggo smoothed a hand down his white shirt. "The angels warned me you like to poke around in their investigations. You'd be wise to stop prodding at something you don't understand."

"Tempest will prod what she likes." Rhett's growl was deep in his chest.

"Yes! I'll prod what I like. I like to prod things." My nose wrinkled. That didn't sound right. "I mean, there's nothing wrong with me asking a few questions. I have my reason for wanting to find out who killed John."

"And what would that be?" Viggo raised an eyebrow. "Worried we might start looking at members of your family?"

I decided to use his tactics on him. "What evidence have you got that John was involved with dark magic?"

Viggo inclined his head as if acknowledging what I'd done. "He was in possession of dark potions."

"He planned to use dark magic here?" I asked.

"Or he'd planned to sell them to somebody," Rhett said. "It could be a deal gone wrong."

"Is that true?" I asked Viggo. "John got on the wrong side of a dark magic user?"

"All possible theories and ones we're looking into," Viggo said. "And as you said, there was dark magic used on that snake who crushed him. Although, by the time the scene had been trampled over by so many people and animals, there was no useful evidence to gather. Your interference has hindered our progress."

"If I knew the Magic Council was coming to fix this mess, I'd have been more discreet," I said.

Viggo chuckled darkly. "Of course, you would."

"What connection did John have to Fur Baby Emporium?" I asked.

He shrugged. "That's also something we're investigating. At a guess, I'd say the store was a quiet, out of the way place. No one would think to look there for dark spells. Familiars use positive magic. If there was a deal going down that involved dark magic, what better place to do it? No one would suspect a thing."

"Who are you looking at in connection to the murder?" I asked.

"So many questions," Viggo said. "I should recommend to the angels that you join them in an official capacity. Although, then your talents outside of Willow Tree Falls may be limited. I hear you enjoy solo missions to capture demons who flee."

"I occasionally take on some freelance work," I said. "But I'm certain the angels won't want me on their team in an official capacity. For one thing, I lack a set of wings. Only angels join the force."

"Still, your input on previous cases hasn't gone unnoticed," Viggo said. "As much as Dazielle complains, you have your uses."

"What does she say?"

He grinned. "It's probably best if you don't know all the details."

I could imagine the grim picture Dazielle painted of my involvement in past investigations.

"We've had deaths in the village before," I said. "What's so special about John that the Magic Council has come to take a look?"

Viggo tipped back on his heels. "What makes you think there's anything special about him? We're doing due diligence."

"Because you're here," Rhett said. "You don't roll out of bed for the small cases. You only take on jobs that enhance your reputation."

"Well observed," Viggo said. "Perhaps I knew the victim. I want to make sure whatever happened is discovered quickly and justice done."

My eyes narrowed. That sounded false. "Did John work for the Magic Council?"

"That's enough questioning for one day," Viggo said. "As much as I appreciate the assistance you give the angels when they're struggling, this little interrogation of yours is over."

"Maybe I can help," I said. "You've said I have my uses."

"Not to me. I'm here to do a job and intend to do it as quickly as possible. You standing in my way isn't assisting," Viggo said.

I glanced at Rhett, and he lifted his chin. I'd pushed my luck far enough, but Viggo hadn't convinced me about anything.

There was something going on here that linked John to the Magic Council, and it wasn't simply the fact Viggo might have known John.

"Good day, Miss Crypt, Mr. Blackthorn." Viggo strolled away.

"Did any of that sound truthful to you?" I asked Rhett.

He grunted. "Maybe two percent of it."

"Have you got time for a coffee?"

"Sure. What's on your mind?"

"This murder." I grabbed my purse and discovered Bandit had climbed back in and was snoozing.

We walked back to the village with Wiggles and stopped at Bite Me.

"Hi, Tilly." I waved a hand in greeting. "Two coffees and two slices of whatever you've got that's delicious, please. Oh, and something for Wiggles."

Wiggles had to stay outside. Tilly didn't like pet fur in the customers' food. Bandit was still in my purse and had fallen fast asleep. I gently placed the purse on the floor and left her to her slumber.

Tilly walked over with the coffees and two slices of lemon drizzle cake. "How's everything going?"

"We've just had an interesting encounter with someone from the Magic Council," I said. "We think they're here because of the murder in Abigail's store."

Her eyes widened. "The dead guy must be someone high up if the Magic Council is getting involved. What do you know about it?"

"Not enough," I said.

She grinned. "You'll get to the bottom of it." She turned to the counter and tutted. "I wish I could stay and chat, but I have to go. Customers waiting."

I sipped my coffee as I turned over the possibilities in my mind. "As soon as I heard his name was John Smith, I got suspicious about this murder."

Rhett nodded. "It's a common name. It's also an excellent name to hide behind if you've got something you don't want people to know."

"John turns up in the village, messes around in Abigail's store, and winds up dead in the store room that same night," I said. "No one knows what he was doing here. I've not even been able to find out where he was staying."

"I can ask the gang to look around and see if he was hiding out somewhere," Rhett said. "The nights have been warm. He could have set up a base in the forest if he wanted to keep a low profile."

"I don't think he's slumming it in the forest or hiding out in a cave," I said. "The suit he wore was designer, and his shoes looked new. He was staying somewhere."

"He could have been trying to start a new life in the village," Rhett said. "Whatever trouble he was in might have meant he had to relocate fast, change his name, and start over."

"But the trouble he was in found him," I said. "And whatever trouble it was, it has him linked to the Magic Council."

Rhett ate some of his cake. "What if it's not so much trouble? Viggo's story about dark magic could be a lie. What if John worked for the Magic Council?"

"John came to the village because he was investigating a case?"

"Viggo Blowhard only comes in on the big cases," Rhett said. "He wouldn't be here unless John had some big lead. Maybe Viggo wanted to snatch the glory and claim the case as his own."

"Or, could John have stumbled on some Magic Council secrets? The Council took him out, and Viggo's here to smooth things over and pin the murder on someone else."

"Also possible. Viggo's here either to hush up John's murder or take the glory for the case he was working on."

"A case that got him killed," I said. "That's assuming John even worked for the Magic Council."

Rhett nodded. "I think this murder is linked to something bigger. Something the Magic Council won't want to get out."

"Which means, I've been looking at this all wrong. Trixie and Abigail can't be involved. If John worked for the Magic Council and was killed because of his ties to them, it's unlikely that anyone in the village is a suspect."

My gut clenched. What about Raine? Aurora said her new job was something official that she kept quiet about. Could she be involved with the Magic

Council and this was all linked? Could she really have had something to do with John's murder?

Rhett tapped the back of my hand. "I sense hard thinking going on behind those beautiful eyes."

"Muddled thinking. This murder is linked to something much bigger than a jealous fight." I bit my lip. "And I'm worried it might track back to a member of my family."

His eyebrows rose. "Do you know who?"

"Unfortunately, I do."

Raine was definitely not in the clear just yet.

Chapter 12

We finished our coffee and cake before I headed out to speak to Raine again. Wiggles was by my side, and Bandit was still asleep in the purse.

Worry churned through me as I began to join the pieces together. First off, there was John arriving in the village and no one knew anything about him. Secondly, Viggo was here to investigate his murder. Thirdly, there was the possibility Raine also worked for the Magic Council in some secretive position. This all had to be connected, but I wasn't sure how.

And what about Viggo's revelation that John was linked to dark magic? Maybe John had gone rogue and the Magic Council was after him. Could the Council have orchestrated this murder and Viggo was here to conceal their involvement?

"Tempest! Have you got a minute?"

I looked around to see Axel's sister, Foxglove, striding toward me. "Sure. What's up?"

"I heard you're looking into that guy's murder."

"News travels fast."

She grinned. "Axel mentioned that you assist the angels with their investigations. Although, he might have put it a little differently than that."

"Sometimes I assist, and sometimes I get dragged into it," I said. "I mainly help out, so innocent people don't get put away. Do you know something about the guy who was murdered?"

"I'm not sure if this is useful information, but he was involved with one of the women who works at that animal store. She's the pretty one with the dark hair and the eastern European accent. Do you know the one I mean?"

"Trixie! Sure, I've talked to her."

Foxglove shrugged. "It's probably nothing, but I was out late the night that guy was killed, and I saw them together. They looked pretty cozy, wrapped in each other's arms like lovesick teenagers. I mentioned it to Axel, and he seemed surprised. He said Trixie's dating the mayor. Have I got that right?"

"Sounds about right." My mouth twisted to the side. This wasn't new information, but it did confirm Trixie was more involved with the victim than she'd let on when I'd quizzed her.

"Should I tell the angels?" Foxglove asked. "I don't want to get somebody in trouble if she's not involved, but it seemed odd that she was fooling around with this guy behind her boyfriend's back, and he's dead the next day."

"The angels might find the information helpful." I'd told Trixie I'd keep quiet about what I knew, but that didn't mean somebody else couldn't let slip to the angels that she could be involved. While they investigated Trixie's connection to John, I could puzzle through just how entangled the Magic Council was in this murder.

"Only if you think it would be useful," she said. "Axel said you run rings around the angels, and they hate it."

I grinned. "It's fun to taunt them a little now and again."

"I bet. I'll drop by the station and let them know what I saw."

"You and Axel should come by the club one evening. I want to hear about all the awful things he did when he was a kid and all the embarrassing stories you have about him."

"Hah! I've got loads of those. It's a date. I'll see you there soon." She raised a hand and walked away.

That information was another mark against Trixie, but I couldn't help but think this had more to do with the Magic Council than a hot date gone wrong. If John had worked for them, the chances were this was a bigger mystery than I'd first realized.

Maybe I should keep away. The Magic Council had been known to use lethal force to get rid of a problem. But before I left this alone, I had to make sure Raine wasn't involved.

I headed to the cemetery with Wiggles and Bandit and wandered through the open wrought-iron gates.

A yawn came from my purse, and Bandit poked her head out.

"Good sleep?" I asked.

"The best." She blinked and looked around. "I sleep a lot now that I'm fur covered. Where are we?"

"The cemetery," I said.

"Let me out. I need to stretch my legs again."

"Be careful." I opened the purse and ducked to let Bandit hop onto the ground. "Sometimes, the demons poke their heads out for a look around."

"It would be terrible if they grabbed you," Wiggles said.

She hissed at him. "I'm surprised they haven't already taken you. You're so slow on those stubby paws, a one-eyed, one-legged demon with blunt claws could pick you off."

"They love me," Wiggles said. "I'm part of their gang, so watch your step, furball. This is my territory you're in."

Bandit shook out her fur and stalked off.

"Do we really need to keep her around?" he asked.

"Not too much longer, but she's been helpful. Once we figure out what happened at Abigail's store, we'll get Bandit a permanent home."

"One far away from here," he said.

I walked to the enormous pale gray stone crypt my family used to store their demon hunting equipment. The door was open, and as I poked my head in, I spotted Granny Dottie sitting in a deck chair with a plate of sandwiches on her lap.

She sat upright and grinned. "Tempest! This is a nice surprise."

"Hi. You all alone?"

"Not for long. Your grandpa forgot his book. He's just headed back to the house to grab it. Keep me company until he gets back." She patted the empty chair beside her. "You can share my sandwiches if you like."

"Did someone say sandwiches?" Wiggles looked inside the crypt, a hopeful expression on his face.

Granny Dottie pulled off a piece of sandwich and tossed it to him, which he caught in the air and swallowed in a single bite.

I took a sandwich from her plate and checked inside. It was salad. "Has Mom got you on a health kick again?"

"She does her best to stop us from getting too slothful," Granny Dottie said. "Don't worry. There are chips down there, and I have dessert. I compromised on the salad sandwiches. They're not so bad if you put enough mayonnaise in them."

I grinned and took a bite of the sandwich. "I've heard about Raine's new job. It sounds exciting."

She slid her gaze my way. "Is that so?"

"How long has she been doing it?"

"That's not for me to say." Granny Dottie shifted in her seat.

"I never thought a Crypt witch would work for the Magic Council," I persevered. "I bet the benefit package is great. Lots of holiday? Free healthcare and dental?"

She simply grunted and stuffed half a sandwich in her mouth.

I leaned closer. "Come on. You can tell me. What's she up to? Raine's not a Magic Council kind of witch."

"It sounds like you already know exactly what your cousin is up to. Why should I know any more than you do?"

I sighed. "Truth be told, I don't know everything, but I'd like to. I'm worried she might be connected to this murder. You've heard about what's happened at Abigail's store, right?"

Granny Dottie's eyebrows shot up. "Why is Raine connected to that?"

"I don't know for certain she is, but someone from the Magic Council has shown up in the village, and he's investigating the murder. If Raine's also working for the Magic Council, then maybe it's all connected."

Granny Dottie was silent.

"Now that I think about it, it was kind of weird that she suddenly announced a last-minute visit. It usually takes weeks of coordination before she can drop in and see us. Raine's always so busy," I said.

She rubbed crumbs off her fingers. "What Raine does is her business. I never interfere."

"You always interfere," I said. "Do you think she's involved in this murder?"

"Where is everybody?" Bandit yelled.

I shook my head. "We're in the crypt, Bandit."

"Who's Bandit?" Granny Dottie asked.

"She's a pain in my—"

"I've arrived." Bandit strutted through the open door. She looked around the crypt, and her nose wrinkled. "I smell death."

"A new pet?" Granny Dottie leaned forward.

"No." Wiggles bared his teeth. "A troublemaker."

Granny Dottie's eyes sparkled. "What a cutie. Come here, puss." She held out her hand.

Bandit regarded her calmly before turning and walking in the opposite direction.

"I told you," Wiggles said. "Never trust an animal who insists on showing you their butt all the time."

Granny Dottie lowered her hand. "That's not your average talking cat, is it?" She looked at me.

"Bandit was found at the scene of the murder," I said. "She led us to the body. I took her home, did a few spells, and suddenly she can talk. Bandit's a fairy. She thinks she was changed into a cat by the victim."

"How fascinating," Granny Dottie said. "Bandit, would you like to return to your original form?"

That got her attention faster than me saying ripe pineapple. Her tail whipped up, and she hurried over. "Absolutely. Change me back. Can you really change me back? I'm so sick of licking myself, thinking chasing my tail is fun, running after anything that moves, and wanting to find small cardboard boxes to squeeze myself into. Change me back! Change me back! Change me back! Meoooowwww."

"Hold on to your fluffy breeches for a second." Granny Dottie chuckled. "We can try a few spells and see if something breaks. If the magic holding you in that form didn't disperse when the spell caster died, it could be a permanent spell."

Bandit groaned. "I can't stay as a cat forever. I have a life to go back to. A life that involves being able to open jars and not rely on other people to feed me."

"Do you remember your life before you turned into a cat?" I asked.

"Just flashes. Now and again, I get a memory. My life as a fairy was amazing. I just know it."

"Where are you from?" Grannie Dottie asked.

"I wish I knew," Bandit said. "Every time I think I've caught onto something from my past, it slips through my paws. A cat brain is an unfocused one."

"Let's see if I can help with that," Granny Dottie said. "Even if you remain a cat forever, you'll still maintain most of your former characteristics and memories, even if it takes a little time to return."

"So, as a fairy, she was also rude, evil, and prone to hysterical outbursts when she didn't get her own way?" Wiggles asked.

"Ignore the hound," Bandit said. "Try your spells on me. Whatever it takes. I can't be a cat forever."

Granny Dottie shrugged. "Come closer. I need to make contact with you." She placed her hands on either side of Bandit's head and closed her eyes. A pulse of blue magic streamed from her palms.

Nothing happened. Bandit remained the same.

She removed her hands and tilted her head as she studied the cat. "How interesting."

"I feel the same," Bandit said.

"That's because you are," Granny Dottie said. "My instinct was right. I'm not sure you can be changed back."

"Nooooooo! I have to be changed back. You're a powerful witch. I can sense that. Try again."

"Very well. We could try this." Her hands wrapped around Bandit's head again, and beams of yellow light flickered across her skin.

Bandit remained as fluffy as ever.

Granny Dottie puffed out a breath and sat back in her seat. "This is most unusual. Whoever put this spell on you knew what they were doing. They wanted you to stay like that forever. What did you do to make them so angry they decided you're to spend the rest of your life as a cat?"

"She breathed," Wiggles muttered.

"I have no idea," Bandit said glumly. "Cat brain, remember? But I get along with everyone. I make friends easily."

"I've yet to see proof of that," Wiggles said.

"Anyone apart from dogs." Bandit growled at him.

"It was definitely John who put this spell on you?" I asked. "Maybe you've gotten muddled and the magic user is still alive. If you can figure out who it is, you can go to them and ask them to change you. Figure out your differences, so you can get back to your fairy form."

Bandit rubbed a paw over one ear. "And if I had those clear memories, I'd do just that. I'm certain it was John who did this to me."

"Then get used to being a cat," Granny Dottie said. "It's not a bad life. You get lots of strokes and can chase things around the floor. Maybe Cora will take you. She was complaining that there might be mice in one of the kitchen cupboards. A cat would deal with that."

"I can deal with any mice," Wiggles said swiftly. "We don't need this cat in our lives. I'll go to Cora's right now and deal with the mouse problem."

"Hang on," I said. "Let's not worry about mice, cats, or anything else. There are three familiars in that house who should see off the mice. We're trying to figure out what happened to John. And I'm certain it has something to do with the Magic Council."

Granny Dottie grabbed another sandwich.

I held her arm down. "Less eating, more talking. What's up with Raine? When I spoke to her the other night in the club, she straight-up lied to me and got Azura to cover for her."

Granny Dottie's expression turned pained. "It's not for me to say."

"How about I guess? You can confirm if I guess correctly. That way, you're not actually telling me anything."

She sighed. "Very well."

"Raine works for the Magic Council?"

She nodded.

"Doing something she doesn't want people to know about?"

Another nod.

"She's hunting criminals," Wiggles said.

"She'll find a lot of those inside the Magic Council," I said.

Granny Dottie snorted a laugh.

My eyes widened. "Oh! I get it. Raine's looking for corruption among Magic Council employees."

Granny Dottie nodded again.

"Which would need to be hush-hush. She's spying on her colleagues. If they found out, she'd be out of a job because no one trusted her."

"Fine! You guessed," she said.

"How come you know if it's such a secret?" I asked.

"I know somebody who knows somebody, who saw Raine at the Magic Council. I asked her about it, and she swore me to secrecy." Granny Dottie glanced around. "Sometimes, being on the inside of an organization like that means you can change it. You know my thoughts on the Magic Council. I've lost dear friends because of their shady behavior.

Having Raine on the inside means corruption can be minimized."

"Raine's a sort of anti-corruption agent," I said.

"I didn't say that," Granny Dottie said. "But if that's what she is doing, then it's admirable. It also means nobody can know about it. If less scrupulous Council members learn of her work, she'll be in trouble."

"So, what's the connection to this murder?" I asked. "Raine knew John. She was seen arguing with him before he died, yet she lied about it. Why's she being so elusive? Was she investigating John?"

"I can't answer that," Granny Dottie said. "And you shouldn't question Raine. You don't want to blow her cover."

"But she looks guilty," I said.

"Nonsense. Raine's innocent. She has nothing to do with killing this person."

I wasn't convinced of her innocence. Raine was involved, and I had to know why.

If I couldn't get Granny Dottie to talk, and Raine wasn't going to reveal anything, I'd have to try somebody else.

"Stop thinking Raine's guilty and help me eat these sandwiches," Granny Dottie said. "She's a good girl."

I opened my mouth to ask another question, but Granny Dottie shoved in a whole sandwich and glared at me.

I shrugged and chewed my food. I knew what my next step was. I had to speak to Azura, see what she knew about her sister's involvement with the Magic

Council, and learn just how tied up in this murder mystery Raine really was.

Chapter 13

The music in Cloven Hoof had me swaying as I served drinks and handed out dried mushrooms. We were short on bar staff this evening, but I was happy to lend a hand. It never felt like work when I was doing something I loved.

"Wow! It's busy tonight." Azura appeared by the bar, accompanied by my sister.

I'd deliberately invited Azura here this evening. It was the perfect opportunity to chat about Raine and learn what she knew about her connection to John.

I placed a double lemon shot and a bowl of mushrooms in front of her. "We're doing a special on house cocktails this evening. It's always popular."

Azura popped a mushroom in her mouth. "Thanks. These are great."

"Where's Raine tonight?" I knew exactly where she was. I'd convinced Granny Dottie to take Raine with her on the late shift at the cemetery, so I got some alone time with her sister.

"Busy. Guarding your demons," Azura said. "Granny Dottie said she wanted to show her a few new moves. I offered to go along, but she only wanted Raine."

"Granny Dottie's funny like that." I ignored the raised eyebrows from Aurora. She was in on this too.

I discreetly topped up Azura's glass every time she took a sip. With a bit of luck, it would loosen her tongue and she might let something slip.

"I'm just going to the powder room. Back in a few." Aurora nodded at me before walking away.

I was just about to start questioning Azura when Axel and Foxglove strolled into the bar.

"Hey! How's everything going?" he asked.

My eyes narrowed. I didn't need any interruptions. I had a cousin to interrogate.

"Good. What can I get you?" I asked.

"A shot of Colombian dwarf whiskey and some of those lemon drops will be good." Axel nodded at Azura. "Enjoying your stay in Willow Tree Falls?"

"Sure, what's not to like?" Her gaze ran over Axel. "Especially if you're going to ask me to dance later."

I sucked in a breath as I waited for Axel's response. He'd better not mess this up.

"That's flattering, but I promise there are guys out there a lot more worthy of your interest than me," he said.

My eyebrows shot up. Axel was turning her down. I wanted to high-five him. Not that there was anything wrong with my cousin; she was cute and fun, but I wouldn't have let him get away with breaking Merrie's heart.

Foxglove snorted a laugh. "What he means is, he's not available." She nodded in the direction of

Merrie, who was serving customers at the other end of the bar.

"Oh, that's a shame." Azura shrugged. "She's a lucky lady."

"I happen to agree with you," Axel said.

Foxglove elbowed him in the ribs. "She's not that lucky. She has to put up with your massive ego."

He chuckled and glanced at me. "How are things going with the investigation into that guy's murder?"

"How should I know?" I placed his drinks down.

Axel grinned and sipped his whiskey.

I lifted a hand. He knew me too well. "As far as I know, the angels don't have much to go on. Nobody knew the guy. Although, I heard he was talking to Raine before he died." My gaze went to Azura to see her reaction.

"Did they know each other?" Axel turned to Azura.

"Nope. And I can't think why anyone would claim they were talking," she said. "We don't know him."

"Is that what Raine told you?" I asked. "She said she'd never met the guy?"

"She hasn't really talked about it," Azura said. "Why would she? It's not as if they arranged to meet up here. We came to see you guys. You know, hang with the family."

"The way you're talking, Tempest, anyone would think you're trying to implicate Raine in this," Axel said.

"Not for a second. Raine's not a killer," I said sharply. I was allowed to have doubts about my own cousin, but no one else could.

Azura pressed her lips together. "Actually, you're not the only one asking questions like that. A guy in a flashy suit was quizzing me earlier."

"What guy?" I asked.

"Not sure. He smelt a bit of garlic," Azura said. "He was short, stocky, and pretty arrogant. He said he works for the Magic Council and is here because he knew the guy who was killed in Abigail's store."

My pulse sped up. "What else did he tell you?"

"Not much. He was asking a lot of questions, though," Azura said. "I didn't have anything to tell him. He kept coming back to Raine and asking what her connection was to the dead guy, but I couldn't help. Why does everybody think they knew each other?"

"Maybe the Magic Council knows something we don't," I said.

"The Magic Council knows nothing," Axel said. "They're annoying with all their rules and regulations. They have no real power."

"You've got that right," Foxglove said. "They're most effective when sitting around a table discussing when to schedule their next meeting."

Axel laughed. "Not like half-demons. Now, if we were in charge of the place, things really would be more fun."

Foxglove nodded. "The Magic Council is only interested when someone is bending their out-of-date rules. Maybe the guy who was killed came to their attention because he was doing that."

"There's a rumor dark magic is linked to his death," I said. "Is that reason enough to get them investigating?"

"Dark magic?" Foxglove tilted her head. "What was he into?"

"Nothing that I could see," I said. "At least there was nothing obviously dark about him when I found his body. That's just what Viggo from the Magic Council said. That must be the guy who was speaking to you, Azura."

"Oh, yeah. I remember him saying that was his name."

"I'll make sure to stay out of Viggo's way. He sounds like no fun," Axel said.

"Good plan," Azura said. "He was a bit of a jerk."

Axel finished his drink. "I'm going to check in with Merrie. You coming?" he asked Foxglove.

"Sure. Right behind you." She nodded at us before strolling away with her brother.

I gave Azura another drink. "I'm worried about Raine if the Council is asking questions about her. You're sure she was with you on the night of John's murder?"

Azura knocked back the drink, her cheeks glowing. "I've already told you."

"I'd understand if you're covering for her," I said. "I'd do the same for Aurora, especially if it got the angels off her back."

"Sure you would. We all do stupid things to protect the people we love."

My heart kicked. "So, you weren't with Raine all night?"

"I can't vouch for what she did when I was asleep," Azura said.

"You think she snuck out?"

She shook her head. "No, she didn't sneak anywhere. She was in bed most of the night. We're sharing a room at Auntie Cora's, and I'm a light sleeper."

"But you heard her get up and leave during the night?"

Azura glanced around, a frown tugging down her lips. "What if she did go out? It's not so unusual. Raine might have gone out for a couple of hours, but she's always doing that."

"What do you mean?"

"It's her standard behavior," Azura said. "She goes out at odd hours of the night on her own. She never tells me where she goes, even though I've asked loads of times. She simply says she can't sleep and goes out walking. That way, she doesn't bother me by making noise in the apartment."

"And you believe that?"

"Why wouldn't I?"

"Does she have a boyfriend? Maybe she's seeing someone the family won't approve of."

"Like a fallen angel, you mean?" Azura grinned. "No, nothing like that. Raine hasn't dated for a while, and she's a bit of a loner, so she's not going out and meeting friends. I think I annoy her by always hanging around too much. She seems happier with her own company. There's no boyfriend, no BFF. It's just the two of us."

"You think she's going out to get away from you?"

Azura shrugged. "It's possible. She's never said anything, but I sometimes think she keeps me around because she feels sorry for me. We might be sisters, but I don't think she always likes me that much."

My brow wrinkled. "What are you talking about? Raine loves you. These trips out at strange hours aren't because of you."

"She's been doing it for months. I hear her in our apartment. Obviously, we've got our own rooms, but even then, I sometimes hear her creeping out in the middle of the night."

"She's not just going to get ice cream?"

Azura shook her head. "No, although that's what I thought when I first heard her. I even came out of my room a few times, expecting to see her sitting there with a container of ice cream and a guilty look on her face, but she was nowhere to be found. Her boots were missing, and she'd left. When I questioned her the next day, she said she'd just gone for a walk, and she'd be quieter the next time, so she didn't wake me."

"And did Raine really know John?" I asked. "Were you covering for her when you said she didn't know him?"

"Oh, no. I've never seen the guy, and she's never talked about him," she said. "I can't think where they met if she did know him."

"Maybe through her new job."

Her eyes widened. "What do you know about that?"

"Probably about as much as you," I said. "Do you think these late-night walks have something to do with her work?"

"Raine always tells me she just does admin."

"You're not so sure?"

She bit her lip. "Admin shouldn't be that stressful. And you shouldn't get called in at weird hours by your boss to do the filing. Unless..."

I leaned closer. "What?"

"She's having an affair with her boss!" Azura slapped down a hand. "Of course, why didn't I think of that?"

"I don't think it's that." I sighed. "Someone saw Raine and John arguing on the day he died. She's really never mentioned him?"

Azura shook her head. "I don't like where you're going with these questions, Tempest. All I know for certain is that Raine can't be involved with this."

Aurora returned from the bathroom and grabbed her drink. "Is everything good?"

I nodded, but I wasn't sure it was. Why had Raine faked an alibi if she had nothing to hide? What was the deal with all the strange disappearances in the middle of the night when no one could see her?

I had a bad feeling about this. Raine wasn't off the hook just yet. And until I learned otherwise, I'd have to keep investigating what her connection was to John's murder.

Chapter 14

"Wake up!"

I jerked upright out of a wonderful dream involving Rhett and melted chocolate. "What's going on?"

Bandit sat on the edge of the bed, her tail swishing. "Someone keeps knocking at the door downstairs."

I dropped back onto my pillows with a grunt. "What time is it?"

"Nine o'clock. You've missed my breakfast," Bandit said.

"It's too early for visitors." I groaned and flipped onto my stomach. "Everyone knows I'm not a morning person."

Bandit hopped onto my back and started to knead.

"Ouch! Quit it. Those claws are sharp." I rolled over to dislodge the kneading, persistent, pussycat.

She hopped daintily off the bed. "Whoever is at the door isn't going away. They've been there ten minutes. Your dog thinks it's an angel."

I groaned again. What did the angels want with me so early? It couldn't be anything good. I hauled myself out of bed, stuffed my feet into my slippers, and shuffled down the stairs.

I opened the door and blinked up into the pristine, wide-awake face of Dazielle.

Her eyes widened a fraction. "Bad night?"

I glowered at her. "Late night. This had better be an emergency."

"Not really." She held up a bag. "I've brought croissants."

I sighed. She knew how to get on my good side. "You'd better come in." I turned and trudged back up the stairs into the apartment, Dazielle following me.

"Coffee?" I asked.

"If you're making." Dazielle looked around my apartment. "Isn't that the cat from Abigail's store? The one who ran off after the body was discovered?"

I glanced at Bandit, who sat looking demure and innocent on the floor. In my half-awake state, I'd forgotten the angels didn't know she was here.

"I'm sort of fostering her for now. She doesn't have a home."

"It's very short term," Wiggles said. His back was turned to Bandit, and his tone suggested he was less than happy she was still around.

I glanced at Dazielle. Should I tell her about Bandit's ability to talk? Or maybe I should simply pass her on to the angels to deal with. They might like a talking cat with attitude living at the station.

"Do you have plates?" Dazielle asked.

"What for?"

"The croissants."

"We don't need plates." I handed her a couple of paper napkins. "These will do."

She sighed. "Do you have any butter? And jelly?"

"This isn't a café," I said. "Eat the croissants as they come. Although, I do have chocolate spread." I opened the cupboard and pulled out an almost empty jar.

Dazielle wrinkled her nose but took the lid off and sniffed. "Actually, that smells good."

"It goes great with warm croissants." I brought over two full coffee mugs and set them on the counter with milk and sugar before sitting on a stool. "So, why the early morning call?"

"We're making progress on John's murder. I've spoken to a number of people who saw him around the village. No one knows much about him, and we haven't been able to trace where he was from, so he still remains a mystery."

I sipped my coffee. "That's progress?"

Dazielle pursed her lips. "Of a kind."

"What's the deal with Viggo?"

She tensed in her seat. "What do you mean?"

"How did he know John?"

"What makes you think he did?"

She was answering a question with a question. That always made me suspicious. "So, who have you got in the line-up for this murder?"

Dazielle munched a huge piece of croissant and chewed slowly.

Worry ran through me when she didn't answer. "What's going on? Why are you really here? You never include me in cases unless you have to."

She swallowed and patted her chest. "As I said, we're making moves in the right direction to find out what happened to John. I've spoken to Abigail and Trixie and asked around in the stores about him. One person has been drawn to our attention."

"And you're going to tell me who that person is?"

"That's why I'm here," Dazielle said. "We're going to question Raine about what she knows about this murder."

I dropped what was left of my croissant. The angels had finally caught up. I bit my bottom lip. Raine was my cousin, but she was being so weird about this murder.

"You don't seem surprised," Dazielle said. "I expected more of a reaction. That's why I brought the croissants. I thought I might need to placate Frank."

"He's fine. Been on his best behavior since the whole Toby stealing Aurora business. It scared him."

"A scared demon. Whatever next?" Her gaze ran over my face. "What do you know about Raine and John?"

"Nothing. I'm not happy that you're planning on questioning a member of my family about this murder." I had to give Raine some wriggle room. "There are more plausible suspects. Going back to Viggo, you never did tell me why he's here."

She shrugged. "It's on a need-to-know basis."

"Since you're planning on interrogating my cousin, I need to know."

"I meant it's on a need-to-know basis for the angels," Dazielle said. "I expect you've heard that Viggo works for the Magic Council."

"He told me himself. He's investigating something about dark magic and that John was selling it or using it or doing something he shouldn't with it. Does that make sense?"

"Viggo does specialize in hunting dark magic users," Dazielle said. "But there was no evidence on John's body that he used dark magic."

"Hold on. Viggo said there were potions found in his possessions. What about those?"

She tilted her head. "I'm not sure what you mean."

"You don't have them as evidence?"

She wrapped her long blonde plait around her wrist. "I mean, it's possible I haven't seen them. I've been busy with other cases. As far as I know, no dark magic was found in John's belongings. Not that he had any."

Had Viggo lied to me about the dark magic link? "You still don't know where John was staying while he was in Willow Tree Falls?"

"It looked like he wasn't staying anywhere," Dazielle said.

"How come Viggo found these potions?" I said. "Did he figure out where John was staying and decided not to tell you?"

"That would be unhelpful. He wouldn't do that."

I arched a brow. "You don't think someone from the Magic Council is lying to you, do you?"

She smirked but shook her head. "I'm not sure what Viggo's doing. He's the lead on this investigation. If he's withholding evidence, he's doing it for a good reason. The Magic Council has every right to come investigate a murder."

"But they don't," I said. "They don't turn up every time someone dies and investigate. Otherwise, there'd be no point in having you here."

She pursed her lips. "True enough. Viggo mentioned knowing the victim. Perhaps that's why he's taken an interest in this case."

I still wasn't buying that possibility. This was connected to the Magic Council, and it had something to do with John and his involvement, but was it because he worked for them and had gone rogue, or was he about to expose a Magic Council secret and they'd gotten rid of him?

And there was still the worrying fact Raine was doing hush-hush work for the Magic Council and just so happened to be here at the same time as John. It all had to be connected, but I still wasn't sure how.

I needed to buy Raine more time. "Have you spoken to Abigail about her alibi?"

"Of course. Since the body was found in her store, it made sense to rule her out as a suspect after checking the facts."

"And you're happy to do that? She convinced you she's innocent?"

"I know you've been asking around," Dazielle said on a sigh. "I don't know why I bother to tell you to keep out of these cases."

"Neither do I. Blame my naturally curious nature," I said. "What do you think of Abigail's alibi?"

"I've heard better," Dazielle said, "but she didn't do anything out of the ordinary. She always shuts the store at eight and goes home. Occasionally, she'll go to the diner for something to eat, and she goes to a book club twice a month, but it was normal for her to shut the store and go home alone."

"And that's what she told you?"

"Do you know otherwise?"

"You might like to ask what she was doing sneaking around late at night with loads of boxes," Bandit said.

Dazielle's head whipped around. "Who said that?"

I shook my head. Bandit had just exposed herself. "There's something I've been meaning to tell you."

Her gaze whipped back to me. "Go on."

"Well, the cat who led me to John's body, she's a bit more than just a cat."

"She's a nightmare," Wiggles muttered.

"It was the cat who just talked?" Dazielle jabbed a finger at Bandit.

"I sure did," Bandit said.

"And why are you only telling me this now?" Dazielle asked, her attention on the cat.

"Bandit's a fairy," I said. "She believes John used a spell on her and turned her into this cat."

"And you haven't changed back?" Dazielle asked. "Even though John's dead?"

"As you can see, I'm still one hundred percent cat," Bandit said, "from my fluffy ears to my annoying tail."

"Wait! Does that mean you saw the murder?" Dazielle asked. "You know who killed John?"

"No idea," Bandit said. "I followed my nose, and it led me to his body. Whoever killed him left hours before I arrived."

Dazielle slumped in her seat. "I thought we were onto something for a second."

"Bandit's right about Abigail," I said. "She isn't as innocent as she appears to be."

"It's true." Bandit settled her tail around her. "The night of the murder, I saw her leaving Willow Tree Falls. She made several trips across the barrier and came back with a load of boxes, which she left in the store."

"She didn't mention that in her statement. Did you see her with John that night?" Dazielle asked. "Was he helping her?"

Bandit shook her head. "I didn't see them together, but I wasn't around all the time. Whatever she was doing that night, she didn't want anybody to see her. She kept to the shadows and kept looking around as if expecting someone to ask what she was doing. She was nervous."

Dazielle frowned. "Okay, so that is suspicious, but if she was nowhere near John—"

"She was in the store," I said. "And Bandit didn't see her the whole time. I also saw Abigail and John arguing the day he died. Maybe John came back and tried to let the familiars loose again. Abigail made sure he couldn't touch them ever again. She's protective of her familiars. She even sleeps with a snake!"

"That doesn't sound all that likely," Dazielle said.

"More likely than my cousin did it," I said. "And what about Trixie?"

"I've already heard from Foxglove about Trixie's late-night activities with the victim," Dazielle said.

"I've spoken to her. She admits they met up for a brief liaison, but that was it."

"A lover's quarrel is a powerful motive for murder," I said. "Don't be too quick to pin this on Raine, not when Abigail and Trixie have lousy alibis and decent reasons for wanting John dead. And don't forget his body turned up in Abigail's store room. They'd both have access. Raine wouldn't."

Dazielle rubbed her forehead. "I'm not chasing after the mayor's girlfriend with so little to go on."

"So, chase after Abigail," I said. "Ask her what she was doing that night."

"I will," Dazielle said. "But I'm still speaking to Raine. She was seen arguing with the victim. And, after much persuasion, Azura admitted that Raine wasn't with her for part of that evening. It's possible your cousin left your mom's house and went to meet John. That meeting ended badly."

The same worrying thought had occurred to me, but I wasn't telling Dazielle that. "What reason did they have to meet? Why would Raine speak to John?"

"That's what I intend to find out," Dazielle said. "Your cousin's lying, and she's getting other people to cover her back. If she's not careful, Azura will be dragged into this too and charged."

"With what?"

"An accessory to murder." Dazielle lifted a hand. "I'm simply here out of courtesy. I wanted you to know what we had planned. Raine's being taken in for questioning, and there's nothing you can do about it."

I glowered at her. If she truly believed that, she really didn't know me at all.

Chapter 15

The second Dazielle left the apartment, I raced to the snow globe down in the bar and activated it, making contact with Mom.

"Mom! Can you hear me?" I said. "You need to get Raine out of the house, right now."

Mom's face briefly appeared before she turned and started talking to someone out of sight.

"What's going on?" I asked.

Her image loomed back into view. "Nothing good!" She looked away again. "Be careful! And you don't need to be so rough with her." She sighed as she turned back to me. "The angels are taking Raine in for questioning over this murder. They think she did it."

My fingers flexed. Dazielle had been sneaky. She hadn't come here out of courtesy to let me know what the angels were planning; she'd been distracting me. She knew what I'd do if I learned they were taking Raine in for questioning. She'd come here with her warm croissants to make sure I was too late to stop this from happening.

"Is Raine okay?" I asked.

"She's fine for now," Mom said. "Auntie Queenie's going crazy, though. She's been yelling at the angels and is chasing them along the garden path as we speak. They'll arrest her if she's not careful. I need to go before any more family members end up behind bars." She disconnected before I could ask any more questions.

I leaned against a stool, my blood heating over Dazielle's deceit. Although I wasn't happy with what she'd done, I was conflicted. Raine was concealing things. She must have realized she couldn't get away with it for long, and the angels would become suspicious when they discovered her lies, just like I was.

I stomped back up the stairs and into the apartment before slumping onto the couch.

Bandit bounced up and peered at me, her nose an inch from mine. "What are we doing now?"

"You're getting off the couch," Wiggles grumbled. "Even I'm not allowed on there."

"That's because you shed fur," Bandit said.

I waved a hand in the air. "No bickering, you two. We need to figure out what's going on with Raine. You know what the angels are like when they set their sights on a suspect."

"How well do you know your cousin?" Bandit asked. "Could she have done this?"

"She's no killer," I said. "But something's going on at the Magic Council, and she's involved."

"Dazielle didn't bring me a croissant." Wiggles thumped a paw on the floor.

"I'll get you one later," I said. "Everyone up. I need to go to Angel Force and see what's happening with Raine."

A frustrating hour later, the angels had made it clear I wasn't getting anywhere near my cousin. They were holding her for questioning, and no one was permitted in to see her.

That included Auntie Queenie, who was sitting next to me in the reception with a scowl on her face.

"You know she didn't do this," Auntie Queenie said. "The angels are making a mistake as usual."

I nodded. "Of course, they are."

"Raine's here to visit with the family. Nothing else."

Wiggles rested his head on her knee. "We'll get her out."

She petted his head. "Good boy. You're right. Raine won't be in here for long."

I glanced at her. "What do you know about her new job?"

She turned in her seat. "Not much. Raine told me it involves a lot of admin, but the pay's good."

"It's just admin?"

She was silent for a long second. "Why? Do you think her job has something to do with this?"

"I'm not sure," I said.

"It's not possible. An administrator working at the Magic Council wouldn't be sent out to assassinate someone."

"But they do have assassins. We know that. We had a visit from one not so long ago."

Her lips pressed together. "My daughter isn't an assassin. This is all a big mistake." She raised her voice. "The angels will pay for this. I'll want compensation."

Jophiel stood behind the desk. "If you keep making threats, I'll have to ask you all to leave."

Mom hurried through the door and hugged Auntie Queenie. "Any news?"

"They won't let me in to see her."

"Where's Azura?" I asked.

"Aurora took her to the store. She thought it would be a good distraction," Mom said. "There's no point in everyone waiting here."

"I'm not leaving until the angels let her go," Auntie Queenie said.

"I'll wait with you," Mom said.

"And I'll go check on Azura," I said. "Don't worry. We'll figure this out."

I headed over to Aurora's store with Wiggles and Bandit, to find Azura sitting behind the counter, a grim expression on her face.

"What's going on with your sister?" I strode to the counter. There was no time to sugar coat this. I had to find out everything about Raine's job and how this was linked to John.

Aurora hurried over. "Keep your voice down. You don't want to scare off the customers."

"We're running out of time now that the angels are involved," I said. "Azura, what do you know about Raine's job at the Magic Council? And don't tell me it's admin like your mom just did."

Azura glanced at me before lowering her head. "I know she's not a killer."

"We all know that," I said. "But she's doing a lot more than filing, isn't she?"

"Oh dear. This calls for cookies," Aurora said. "Tempest, be kind." She shot me a warning look before hurrying away.

"Raine's in a lot of trouble," I said. "The angels are closing in, and her false alibi has been discovered. Potentially, you're in trouble too since you covered for her."

"Neither of us killed that guy," she said quietly.

"But Raine was connected to him?"

She shrugged. "It's possible. Ever since she took this job, she's been cagey about what she does. She plays it down, but it's something important at the Magic Council."

"Important how? Did John work for the Magic Council? Maybe he uncovered something he shouldn't and came to the village to hide. Did Raine get orders to hunt him down and bring him back?"

"No, it's not that."

Aurora returned with a plate of cookies. She settled on a seat next to Azura and took her hand. "Take your time. Tempest is only trying to help. We've both been on the wrong side of the angels, so we know they can make a mistake."

"And they're not going to do that with Raine," I said. "But only if you tell us everything you know about her job with the Magic Council."

Azura sighed. "I might not have been totally honest when we spoke at the club. There's no affair with her boss. I believe she goes out at strange times of the night to hunt down people who illegally use magic."

"Just like Tempest hunts demons?" Aurora said.

Azura nodded. "Pretty much. As you know, there are spells and incantations we can't use because the magic is forbidden."

"Raine arrests people for non-compliance of magical law," I said. "That's not so different from a lot of people who work at the Magic Council."

"I don't think that's exactly her role," Azura said. "Like I said, I'm not completely sure, and she always shuts me down when I try to get more information. From what I've managed to find out, she's working as a sort of internal auditor for the Magic Council. She's trying to weed out employees who are misusing magic."

"Wow! That's a serious job," Aurora said.

"And one that won't make her popular," I said. "Investigating people she works with means no one will like her. Everyone at the Magic Council will see her as a potential threat, worried she might uncover something they've done that they're not proud about."

"Which means somebody might want to set her up," Aurora said. "Could that be what's happened here? Someone from the Magic Council learned John and Raine were going to be in Willow Tree Falls at the same time, and they framed her for his murder?"

"It was a lousy frame if that's what they did," I said. "There was no evidence of Raine at the crime scene. If you were planning to frame someone for murder, you'd plant physical evidence, like hair or a bloody footprint. Something obvious."

"Maybe whoever did it thought the argument Raine had with John was enough to make people question her," Aurora said.

"I don't think she was framed." I grabbed a cookie and took a bite.

"We have to find out who killed him," Azura said. "Raine doesn't react well to confined spaces."

"Your mom's at Angel Force," I said. "If anything goes down, she'll be on hand to calm the situation."

"What can we do to prove Raine's innocence?" Aurora asked.

"Find out more about John Smith," I said. "Why was he here? Is John Smith his real name?"

"Doubtful," Azura said.

I tapped my chin. "We need to go to the source. The reason he was sent here."

"You want to contact the Magic Council?" Aurora shook her head. "Are you sure that's a good idea?"

"No, but they must be able to confirm John worked for them and what he did. That would help us find out if he knew Raine. Maybe they worked in the same department. Or, if they didn't, she could have been following him because he was suspected of illegally using magic."

Aurora grimaced. "Be discreet. Otherwise, the Magic Council might start probing into your affairs."

"I definitely don't want to be probed by the Magic Council." I shook Aurora's snow globe. "This could take some time. We're going to need more cookies."

"If I get put on hold again, I'm coming to your office and—" I squeezed my eyes shut as the supposedly calming classical music filtered over the snow globe.

I'd been getting the run around from the Magic Council for almost an hour as I tried to get information about who John Smith was and how he'd come to be in Willow Tree Falls.

Everyone I asked pretended they'd never heard of him and couldn't find any mention of him in their system.

Aurora nudged the almost empty plate of cookies toward me. "Maybe you should give up. You've been passed around seven departments, and no one knows who he is."

"They all claim not to know who he is," I said. "That doesn't mean I believe them. The fact they're not telling me anything only makes me more suspicious that he worked for them, and they don't want anybody to know about it."

"Which means whatever he did had to tread close to being illegal," Azura said. "I've heard rumors the Magic Council employs freelancers to do their dirty work, so if anything backfires, it can't be traced to them."

"And if that's true, John was doing dirty work that got him killed," I said. "He was—"

"You're through to Magical Acquisitions and Evaluations. My name's Francine Finkle. How may I help you?"

"Hi, Francine. I'm looking for a colleague of yours, John Smith," I said. "I was passed from another department to you. They thought you might know who he is." I deliberately wasn't speaking about John in past tense just in case word hadn't gotten around the whole of the Magic Council that he was dead.

There was a second too long of silence. "We don't have anybody by that name working here."

"But you know him?"

"The name's not familiar. Which department does he work in?"

"I don't know," I said on a sigh. "You must have a staff directory. Can you look him up and find out for me?"

"If you need to speak to Mr. Smith, then you must know where he works."

I gritted my teeth. "You'd think so. You'd also think an employee of the Magic Council could help me with an inquiry about someone who works there. I just need to know what John's specialty is."

"As I said, we don't work together." Francine's tone grew cold.

"But you can look him up?"

"Let me put you on hold. I'll see what I can do."

"No! Don't you dare—" The music began again. I shook my head as I disconnected the snow globe.

Azura's bottom lip jutted out. "Thanks for trying, Tempest. That got us nowhere, though."

"It got us somewhere. From the way the employees at the Magic Council behaved, they know John's dead. Maybe they've got a memo that goes around letting them know who got killed on duty and not to talk about it. Every time they looked up his name, they shut down and passed me on as quickly as possible."

"And whatever he was up to, it got him killed," Aurora said.

I looked up as Dominic strolled past the store. "He might be able to help us fill in some of these blanks." I jumped off my seat, raced out the door, and grabbed his arm, spinning him toward me.

His eyes widened before he grinned. "Hey, Tempest. How's it going?"

"Great! Come inside. We've got tea and cookies."

He glanced along the road. "I should be getting back to work."

"Aurora's cookies are amazing." I tugged him closer to the store.

"I guess I can spare five minutes, especially for cookies."

I was happy to share my cookies with Dominic, especially since he was always eager to share any news from Angel Force. Despite Dazielle always telling him to keep quiet when he was around me, he always enjoyed gossiping.

I sat him on the seat I'd vacated and shoved the cookies at him. "So, what's new at Angel Force?"

He took a cookie and bit into it. "Not much. These are great. Did you make them, Aurora?"

She nodded. "I've more time on my hands now that I'm single. I'm getting into baking in a big way."

Dominic swallowed his cookie noisily. "Oh, sure. It's good to keep busy, especially after such an unfortunate... incident."

"Yes, Aurora doesn't have the best of luck with guys," I said. "You look busy over at Angel Force."

"Sure, we're always busy," he said.

"And what about the investigation into John Smith's death?" I asked. "How's Raine doing? I tried to get in to see her earlier, but I couldn't get through."

He tilted his chin. "Ah! Sorry about that. Dazielle's orders."

"Soooooo, are you letting her go soon?" I asked.

"It's not looking good for Raine. I know she's your cousin, but we've got enough to hold her."

"You're not going to charge her?" I glanced at Azura. She'd gone very pale.

"My sister didn't kill that guy," Azura said quietly. "She can get a bit hot-headed at times, but that's a family trait. She didn't know him."

"Raine admitted to us that she planned her visit to Willow Tree Falls at the last minute," Dominic said. "Why do you think that is?"

"Because we have family here, and she wanted to see them," Azura said. "Although, I guess it was a bit weird. We'd planned a chilled-out weekend at the apartment. I'd even gotten in the popcorn and treats. All of a sudden, Raine said we had to come to Willow Tree Falls."

I trod on Azura's foot to shut her up. She was hardly helping her sister by telling Dominic that information.

She glanced at me, and her eyes widened before she clapped her hand over her mouth. She lowered it. "Not that it means anything. We come here whenever we like. I'm sure Raine just wanted to catch up with Mom and everyone else."

"That's right," I said. "It's not a crime to visit family."

Dominic nodded. "Your family is great. It's Raine's bad luck she was here at the same time as John. And if she does have a temper, maybe it got the better of her."

"She might have yelled at him, but she wouldn't have killed him," Azura said.

"Or maybe she didn't yell at him at all." I glared at Azura. What was she trying to do, get the angels to charge her sister with murder?

He tilted his head. "Did your sister tell you she shouted at John? They got into an argument before he was killed?"

I slid in front of Azura, blocking Dominic's view. "We both saw what happened to John. There's no evidence my cousin was there. You can't charge someone without evidence."

He shrugged, and his cheeks grew pink. "It's not rock solid, but we're getting there. We've got enough to hold her while we do more investigation. Dazielle's confident she'll get a confession out of Raine."

Azura squeaked, while Dominic picked up another cookie and began to eat.

This was terrible news. With the angels focused only on Raine, the real killer would get away.

Unless, they already had the real killer.

Had I gotten this all wrong and just wasn't willing to accept Raine was involved in this murder because we were related? I thought I knew her well, but with her secret job and the fact she'd lied straight to my face, I was having doubts.

Were the angels right? Had Raine killed John?

Chapter 16

I peered up at the sky through my apartment window, not liking the look of the gray clouds that hung low overhead the next morning.

I felt stuck. Raine was still being held by the angels, the Magic Council wasn't talking about who John really was and why he'd come to Willow Tree Falls, and I had no solid evidence to pursue another suspect.

I kept bumping up against a brick wall and hadn't yet figured out a way to slam through it and figure out this mystery.

"Are we staying inside and moping around all day?" Bandit asked. She was stretched out on the couch and kept teasing Wiggles by dangling her tail above his bed.

"I'm not moping," I said.

"You've had a face on you like a smacked bum since yesterday," Bandit said.

"I haven't! This is just my face." I glared at her.

"If we are staying in, you need to crack a window open. That dog's been letting off silent gas attacks for hours," Bandit said. "I feel sick."

Wiggles, who'd been doing a great job of faking sleep, rolled over. "Hey! You can't blame me because I have a sensitive stomach."

"You have a disgusting stomach," Bandit said. "I saw you eating out of the trash yesterday. If you had a better diet, you wouldn't stink so bad."

"I smell fine," Wiggles said. "Tempest loves my smell."

My nose wrinkled. It was getting a little pungent in here. "Let's get some food and see Aurora again. She still needs to make a decision on whether she's getting a familiar."

"I could definitely eat." Wiggles rolled off his bed and wandered over to me.

"You can always eat," Bandit said. "That's the problem. You have no restraint."

"I have restraint," he said. "If I didn't, you'd be fried to a crisp by now. Besides, I don't need to hold back when it comes to food. I burn it all off."

"It looks to me like it's all going to fat," Bandit said. "Would you like some ham to go in that roll around your gut?"

He growled at her.

"Enough!" I pulled on my jacket and headed down the stairs with Wiggles and Bandit right behind me. I grabbed my oversized purse off the bar, and Bandit hopped inside, seeming happy to be carried around like I was her personal servant. Typical cat attitude. They'd never forgotten they used to be worshipped as gods in ancient Egypt.

I grabbed three falafel and sweet chili baguettes from the Unicorn's Trough and a bowl of fruit for Bandit before heading to Aurora's store.

She waved at me through the window as we approached.

I pushed the door open and walked in. "Have you had lunch yet?"

"Nope. Actually, I was thinking of closing up for half an hour and grabbing something."

"No need. We got you this."

She grabbed the baguette I held out. "Yum! Looks great."

"I thought we could go back to Fur Baby Emporium," I said. "Are you still thinking of getting a familiar?"

Her eyes widened. "I am. And while we're there, you can talk to Abigail again about John's murder."

I grinned. "Great minds think alike. There's no harm in asking a few more questions. After all, our cousin is still being interrogated by the angels. Maybe Abigail has information that can help get her out."

Aurora unwrapped her baguette and took a bite. "I can only shut the store for half an hour. I won't be able to make a decision in that time, but I would like to look at the owls again."

"Then let's go."

We hurried out the store, and she locked up behind us.

"I thought you'd ruled out owls as your familiar of choice," I said.

"I'm keeping an open mind," Aurora said. "But now that I'm a single woman, I need a familiar who'll not only enhance my magic but act as my protector."

Wiggles loudly cleared his throat. "One protector at your service."

She petted his head. "I know you'll always look out for me, but you belong to Tempest. Besides, I was thinking something a bit bigger and scarier is called for."

"You haven't forgotten that I breathe fire?" he asked.

"And it's charming when you do that," Aurora said. "But I want a familiar who looks physically intimidating. If I'm at the store late and on my own, I want to know I'll be safe. If someone peers in and thinks about doing something they shouldn't, my familiar will stop them in their tracks."

"How about an eagle?" I suggested. "Terrifying looking, killer beak, and claws that will rip a person's heart out."

"Maybe not that terrifying." Aurora grimaced. "Maybe a big dog. I don't know. Would I suit a dog?"

"No more dogs," Bandit said from inside the purse. "That's a terrible idea."

Wiggles cleared his throat again.

Aurora scooped him off the ground and snuggled him. "You'll always be my favorite hellhound. And if I get a dog, you two can play together."

Wiggles snuffled her ear and took a sneaky bite of her baguette. "That's not a terrible idea, but we have to get along. No picking a familiar without my approval."

"That's why you're here," she said. "If I see anyone I like, you can spend time together and see if you can be friends."

"It's a deal," Wiggles said.

We ate our baguettes as we walked the rest of the way to Fur Baby Emporium and headed inside.

"Oh! Look! Puppies." Aurora hurried to a large glass-fronted pen, where three fluffy black puppies played together.

"They're not exactly terrifying," I said. "People will break in to your store to pet them they're so cute."

"They are just to die for," she said. "What breed are they? Maybe they get big when they're older."

"You've spotted my adorable Havanese puppies." Abigail bustled over from the back of the store. "Aren't they sweet?"

"Gorgeous. How big do they get?" Aurora asked.

"Not big. They're perfect apartment dogs." Abigail smiled. "Touch one. See what happens."

Aurora's mouth twisted, but she leaned over and placed a finger on a puppy. A sparkle of red mist shot out.

"What just happened?" I asked.

"They trigger on contact," Abigail said. "It's specific to this breed because they love being close to their owner. This is the perfect familiar to make you confident in your powers."

"That sounds uncomfortably clingy," I said. "What if Aurora takes a holiday without the sparkly pup?"

"Not advised," Abigail said. "These familiars bond strongly to their owner. They've been known to die of a broken heart if their owner isn't constantly attentive. Many magic users with this kind of familiar drape them around their necks. I even had one customer who wore her dog in a papoose. He loved it."

"Oh, maybe they're not for me," Aurora said. "They're so sweet, but I'm looking for a familiar who can stand up for themselves and me."

"A guardian familiar," Abigail said. "That's what you need. I should have anticipated that. Given, well, your recent relationship split."

"You mean, when my fiancé brainwashed me and turned me into a stone dragon?" Aurora sighed.

"Erm, well, yes." Abigail glanced at me as if looking for some support.

I tucked an arm around Aurora's shoulders. "Let's take a look at some guardian familiars. As sweet as these little guys are, they're not right for you. Remember, you said you wanted big and scary."

"Scary!" Abigail shook her head. "I don't breed scary familiars."

"Goliath's pretty scary." I nodded as we passed his tank.

"Only if you know nothing about snakes," Abigail said. "The poor baby is still shaking after everything that was done to him. He might never fully recover from the abuse he suffered."

Aurora peered at Goliath. "I don't want a snake familiar. But I was wondering about a dog."

"An excellent choice. There are several in the back. Right this way." Abigail led us along a row of cages containing an array of chirping birds who sparkled with magic.

She unlocked a door, and we walked into a small, enclosed area that looked set up for training dogs. There were toys scattered around and a couple of food bowls.

"This is the space I let the dog familiars in to give them exercise," Abigail said. "It's secure, so you can give them a good walk around and try out their different personalities. I've got five familiars you might be interested in. They're trained and ready to go."

"I'd like to meet them all," Aurora said.

"Head to the back, and you'll see their pens. It's best to let them out one at a time. They're due some exercise, so they might be a little excitable. If you find one that fits you, you'll know. He'll follow your commands instantly."

I caught hold of Aurora's elbow as she walked toward the pens. "And while you're doing that, I'm going to have a little chat with Abigail."

She nodded. "Okay, I'll see you back here soon. Maybe with a new friend in tow."

We waited a couple of minutes, watching as Aurora let out the first dog. He was a short, stumpy-legged guy with a two-toned black-and-white face. He bounced around and grabbed a ball before dropping it by Aurora's feet.

She smiled at me. "I'll be fine here."

"Shall we leave her to it?" I said to Abigail.

"Good idea. It's important to spend time bonding with a potential familiar." Abigail led the way out of the enclosure and closed the door behind us.

"I expect you've heard what's going on with the investigation into John's murder," I said.

She glanced at me, and her face paled. "A little. I heard Raine's been taken in for questioning."

"She's innocent," I said swiftly. "There are other suspects the angels still need to talk to, but while they've got their focus on Raine, they're not pursuing anyone else."

"Who else do you think they need to speak to?" She straightened a pile of leaflets on the counter.

"You."

Her head shot up. "Why do you think I'm involved?"

"Because you lied about your alibi."

She shook her head. "I didn't. I was at home and asleep when it all happened."

"Lies." Bandit's head poked out of my purse.

"Oh!" Abigail peered at the cat. "It's you. I wondered what happened to that cat. She talks!"

"I do. Greetings from cat land," Bandit said.

She leaned closer. "That's... interesting. Have you always been able to speak?"

"Pretty much, apart from a weird month or so." Bandit glanced up at me. "Tell the story, witch."

Abigail raised her eyebrows and looked at me.

"Bandit's technically not a cat. Well, she is, but she used to be a fairy. She believes John turned her into a cat, and she can't revert to her original form. I used some spells, so I could get her talking."

"And I saw what you were actually doing on the night of John's murder. That's how Tempest knows you lied," Bandit said.

"Well, maybe I did conceal something small." Abigail's nose wrinkled. "That doesn't mean I had anything to do with what happened to John. It was just bad luck he ended up in my store."

"And why was that?" I asked. "Why come here and get himself killed?"

"I can't answer that," she said. "Maybe he thought it was somewhere he could hide."

"How did he get in? There were no signs of a break-in when I walked through the back door," I said.

She looked away. "I have no idea."

I sucked in a breath and lowered some barriers that kept Frank contained. If I couldn't get her to talk, maybe he could.

He eased up my spine in a sticky, hot wave, not seeming in any hurry to get involved.

Bandit's head swiveled slowly toward me. "You smell funny."

"Sort of like Wiggles on a bad day?" I asked.

She hopped out of the purse and skittered across the counter, her fur puffed up. "Worse. What are you doing?"

The birds closest to me chirped in alarm and flapped as they sensed the waking demon.

I kept Frank under control, but it wouldn't do any harm to let him peek through and warn Abigail that she needed to cooperate.

She took a step back, her face blanching. "Now, Tempest, there's no need to get angry. I didn't kill John."

Frank grumbled, the noise echoing around my head. "What are we doing here?"

"All I want is the truth," I said to Abigail. "Tell me what you were doing the night of John's murder, and I'll put Frank back in his cage."

Abigail's gaze cut to the birds that were flapping around in alarm. "Please, my familiars are sensitive.

They don't like it when they come into contact with such dark power. It's not good for them."

"We're in a pet store?" Frank growled.

I ignored him. "Your familiars will come to no harm. Just tell me what happened that night. Bandit saw you leaving Willow Tree Falls. You returned with a load of boxes. What was in the boxes?"

"Nothing." She glanced at Bandit. "The cat's mistaken."

"I don't make mistakes." Bandit's narrowed-eyed gaze slid from me to Abigail. "But maybe you should tell Tempest what she needs to know, so she stops smelling so peculiar."

She pressed her lips together. "Fine, I'll tell you the truth. But please, put Frank away."

I blew out a breath and gently eased him back. He didn't protest. He wasn't at all interested in being surrounded by familiars.

I was glad Aurora was in another room surrounded by the positive magic of so many familiars. It meant he was less likely to detect her and go on the hunt.

"So, what were you doing that night?" I asked.

Abigail swallowed and licked her lips. "I have an arrangement with someone. He helps me with my stock."

"Someone outside the village?" I asked.

"That's right. Familiars are difficult to get hold of, especially ones who've been properly trained. And they're expensive."

"You had familiars in those boxes Bandit saw you with?" I asked.

"Only a few," Abigail said.

"Where do they come from?"

"My contact acquires them from homes they're not suitable for and passes them to me. Some need a little rehabilitation, but I'm always happy to do that. A few weeks with me and they're fully functioning familiars."

"You're handling stolen familiars, so you can get them at a cut price?"

"They're not stolen, just not suitable for their current position." Abigail looked around and clasped her hands together.

"Which is why you meet this contact in the middle of the night and sneak them in the store when no one can see you," I said. "That sounds completely legit."

She sighed and rubbed her forehead. "I love dealing with familiars. I get such satisfaction in finding them their perfect home. What's better than a home in Willow Tree Falls? We have some of the strongest magic users in our community living here. Any familiar would think it was wonderful to move here."

I hoped that story comforted Abigail when she handled the stolen goods. "And this mystery person only gets you familiars?"

She shook her head. "Discounted stock as well. He tells me it falls off the back of a lorry. I don't ask any questions and simply pay. What I do benefits everyone in the village. I can price my stock competitively, so people get a bargain when they come to me. It's one of the reasons I've kept going for so long and am so popular."

"By stealing from other people." I tilted my head. "Not cool."

"I've had no complaints from my many satisfied customers," she said. "That's why I was out late that night. I'd arranged to meet my seller and headed out to pick up my order."

So, Abigail was crooked but maybe not a killer. "You brought the stock back to the store that night?"

She nodded. "I did. I checked on the familiars I'd purchased. There were three of them, two owls and a lizard. They were in good health and just needed settling into their new homes. I did that and then left."

"Did you put the stock in the back room?" I asked.

"I didn't go in there," Abigail said. "I was exhausted. It had been a long day, and I'd only had a couple of hours sleep before I had to head out and pick up my collection. I grabbed the familiars, settled them in, and left the stock on the counter for the next day. You even saw me unloading it when you came in the back door."

I nodded. "John could have been in the store room while you were here. He might have already been dead and was back there when you dropped off the familiars. How did he get in?"

She bit her bottom lip. "As I said, I was tired. Willow Tree Falls is generally a safe place. I could have forgotten to lock the back door. If I had, John could have wandered in. I don't know why he picked my store, but I had nothing to do with his death."

"I need to speak to your contact," I said. "How do I know you're telling the truth?"

Her eyes widened. "I am."

"You lied about your first alibi," I said. "I need confirmation about this one."

"He won't like speaking to you."

"And you won't like me chatting to the angels about what you really did on the night of John's murder."

"No! I don't want them to know. If they learn I'm selling knockoff goods in my store, they might shut me down. What will happen to all my familiars? Tempest, you won't tell them, will you?"

"If you put me in touch with your contact so I can confirm your alibi, I'll keep quiet," I said.

Abigail sighed. "Give me a minute. I need to contact him on the snow globe." She hurried away from the counter.

I looked around for Wiggles. He had his paws on the windowsill and was looking outside. "What do you think of her story?" I asked Bandit.

"It's possible she's being truthful," Bandit said. "The boxes were big enough to hold familiars. And I remember seeing small holes in the side of a couple of them. They could have been air holes."

Abigail returned, her snow globe activated. "I've told him you just need to know about that night. Don't push. I don't want to lose this contact."

"Sure. What's his name?"

"No names," she said. "You check where I was that night, and that's it."

I shrugged. "Fair enough. Hi, Mystery Man. I need you to confirm some details about the whereabouts of Abigail three nights ago."

There was a pause. "Go ahead." His deep voice was laced with caution.

"What time did you meet to hand over the goods you delivered?"

"Just after one in the morning. It's our usual time slot."

"How long did the handover take place?"

"Fifteen minutes."

"And what did you deliver?"

"Tempest," Abigail warned. "That's not relevant."

I pursed my lips. "It is. How do I know you haven't just contacted a friend to cover for you?"

"Three familiars," he said. "Two owls and a lizard. Plus two boxes of assorted leashes, harnesses, and toys. Anything else you need to know?"

It wasn't perfect, but it was good enough. "Thanks. That's it."

The connection on the snow globe died.

"Happy now?" Abigail asked.

I frowned. "Not really. Someone has to know what happened here that night."

"If your cousin isn't involved, what about Trixie?" Abigail asked. "I was telling the truth about seeing her flirting with John when he came to the store."

"Is Trixie working today?" I asked.

"She should be, but she hasn't shown up. If she's not careful, she'll lose her job. I don't care that she's dating our mayor. She can't mess me around. I'm all on my own here."

With Abigail ruled out, Trixie was another possibility, but if this murder was connected to the Magic Council, I thought it unlikely she was involved. Still, another poke at her wouldn't do any harm. "Any idea where she might be?"

"Mannie's probably taken her away for a long weekend of fun." She sighed. "Trixie's a good worker when she's here, but sometimes she lets me down."

There was a shriek and a thud from the room Aurora was in.

"Oh dear." Abigail shot me an irritated look. "I got distracted thanks to your interrogation. I hope your sister's all right." She bustled over and opened the door.

I poked my head inside and laughed. Aurora was on the floor, two dogs bounding around her, alternating between licking her face and hands and chasing each other.

She rolled away and spotted me. "These dogs are too boisterous for me."

"Big tends to be boisterous," I said. "Are you sure you want a big dog as a familiar?"

She swiped a hand across her well-licked cheek as she struggled to her feet. "Maybe I need to rethink things."

"Hey! Something's going on outside." Wiggles bounded over from the window.

"What is it?" I asked.

"Two angels have just flown past," he said. "They're going fast. We should see where they're going."

I took a step toward the door to take a look for myself.

Abigail grabbed my arm. "You will be discreet with what I've told you, right? I don't want the angels finding out what I do here."

"They won't hear it from me." I gestured Bandit to hop into my purse, secured it over my shoulder, tucked my hand through Aurora's elbow, and we left the store.

"So, what's Abigail been up to?" Aurora asked.

"Not murder," I said. "She's got a deal with someone outside the village. She's taking in stolen goods and selling them."

Her eyes widened. "Which means she's not innocent."

"True, but that crime doesn't interest me. Which direction did the angels go?" I asked Wiggles.

"Opposite end of the road." He trotted ahead of us. "I'll show you."

"Let me out." Bandit struggled out of the purse and hopped to the ground. "My nose is better than yours. I'll be able to sniff out the angels."

"I've got this." Wiggles' speed increased.

Bandit matched his pace. "You don't know where you're going."

"I do," he said. "Keep your fuzzy butt out of this." His pace increased, and Bandit trotted along beside him, seeming determined to keep up.

I glanced at Aurora and shook my head. "I don't suppose you want a cat as your familiar?"

"I'm not sure a cat's scary enough," she said.

"I'm much more than a simple cat," Bandit said over her shoulder as she continued to match pace with Wiggles. They were almost running in their efforts to outdo each other.

I sped up to keep up with them.

"What are the angels chasing?" Aurora jogged beside me.

"Nothing good." A worrying feeling flickered through me. Maybe they'd found evidence in the murder investigation. I hoped it didn't lead them back to Raine.

"This way." Wiggles broke into a full out run, and Bandit launched after him, determined not to be outdone.

I raced after them toward a small, whitewashed house with roses around the door. Several angels milled around outside, the front door open.

Wiggles screeched to a halt, narrowly missing slamming into an angel's legs. "I win!"

"It wasn't a race." Bandit slowed to a trot, her tail swishing from side to side.

"It so was. And you're the loser," Wiggles said.

They continued to bicker as I stopped in front of Jophiel. "What's going on here?"

She glanced down at me. "There's been a murder."

"Another one?" My eyes widened.

"Who's dead?" Aurora asked.

"Viggo Blowhard."

Chapter 17

My jaw dropped. "The guy from the Magic Council? Who killed him?"

Jophiel looked down her nose at me. "That's what we're investigating."

"Hey, Tempest!" Dominic trotted down the steps of the house. "You've already heard the news?"

"Is it true?" I asked. "Is Viggo dead?"

Jophiel slid Dominic an angry glance and shook her head.

He ignored her and smiled. "It sure is. He was found not ten minutes ago."

"What happened to him?" I asked.

Jophiel cleared her throat. "Better not say anything else, Dominic."

He pulled back his shoulders. "Oh, right. Of course. Sorry, Tempest. It's an ongoing investigation. I'm sure we'll be able to tell you everything, just as soon as we figure out what happened."

I tried to peer around Jophiel, but she spread her wings to block my view.

I glared at her before backing away with Aurora, Wiggles, and Bandit. "This is amazing news!"

"Not such amazing news for Viggo," Aurora said.

"No. I mean, of course, bad luck for getting himself killed," I said. "But he was killed while Raine's being held by the angels. These murders have to be connected, which means she's innocent."

"Oh! I didn't think about that," Aurora said.

"John worked for the Magic Council, and Viggo definitely worked for them as well. There's no way this is a coincidence. We need to get inside that house." I looked at Wiggles and Bandit. "Can you two go inside and see what's going on?"

"I'll do that," Bandit said. "I'm excellent at being stealthy."

"I'm way better at that than you," Wiggles said. "And I've done this sort of thing before. Tempest trusts me. I can get in and out without anybody noticing."

"How about you go in together?" We didn't have time to stand around arguing over who was better at breaking into a house. "Creep in, see what's going on, and report back. Make sure you don't get spotted."

"As if that will happen." Bandit turned and sprinted around the side of the house, Wiggles right on her furry heels.

"Are you certain you don't want Bandit?" I asked Aurora. "My life used to be much less stressful when I only had one furball in it."

She shrugged. "I'll give it some thought. I hate to leave you, but I have to get back to the store. Will you be okay here?"

"Sure. Get out of here," I said. "I'm sticking around to see what I can find out."

We said our goodbyes, and Aurora hurried away.

I hung around for a few moments as the angels hurried about and soon spotted Dazielle at the front door.

Her gaze speared into me, and she frowned before striding over. "What are you doing here? Come to gloat?"

"About..."

"The murder."

My eyebrows shot up. "Why do you always think I'm involved with every murder in this village?"

"Hmmm, let me think." She tapped her chin. "You have a demon living inside you. You have no respect for the law. You've been caught at more than one murder scene. Need I go on?"

I waved a hand in the air. "This one's not on me. What happened to Viggo?"

"He's dead."

"I gathered that. How? Who did it to him?"

She shook her head and crossed her arms over her chest.

I sighed. This was going well. "At least one good thing's come out of this."

"What would that be?"

"Raine's still in your custody?"

"Correct."

"Then she can't be involved in this murder."

"Maybe not this one," Dazielle said.

My gut clenched. "She's confessed to John's murder?"

There was a long pause. "Not yet."

"And she never will," I said. "Put the pieces together. John and Viggo both worked for the Magic

Council. Now, they're dead. What does that tell you?"

"That somebody doesn't like people who work for the Magic Council."

"That the murders are connected! Therefore, Raine can't have killed John."

"Or she's working with someone," Dazielle said. "She killed John, and her accomplice murdered Viggo."

"Why? Tell me her motive."

"Your sister has a history with the Magic Council," she said, "not all of it good."

My eyes narrowed. Did Dazielle know Raine worked at the Magic Council? "That doesn't mean she'd kill people who worked there."

She lifted her chin. "Do you know Raine has a record? Two counts of affray."

"Again, that doesn't make her a murderer," I said.

"But it does make her a suspect," Dazielle said. "I've caught her lying, she has a record, and her alibi for the night of the murder isn't solid. She's staying in my custody because she appears guilty."

I forced myself to stay calm. "If these murders are linked, and I'm certain they are, she can't be involved. I'm not buying the accomplice theory."

"What about her sister?" Dazielle asked.

"No! No way," I said. "Azura's been with me most of the time."

"Was she with you an hour ago?"

"Was that when Viggo was murdered?"

Dazielle's lips pursed. "That's for me to know."

A trickle of Frank's energy slid up my spine, and I let it. Why did Dazielle always have to be so stubborn?

Her nostrils flared. "Back down, Tempest. Walk away from this."

"Not while you're keeping Raine on the hook for John's murder," I said. "And don't try to fit her up for this one as well. It'll blow up in your face, and you'll be sorry."

"Are you going to make me sorry?" She stepped closer. "Or should I say, Frank? Are you planning on letting your demon out to play?"

"Don't tempt me." I growled and smacked the flat of my palm against her chest.

"Erm, Tempest, maybe you should cool down." Dominic hurried over, concern on his face. "We don't want any trouble."

"Then tell your boss to stop being so hard-nosed." Frank's energy tickled the back of my neck. It was tempting to unleash him on Dazielle. It might knock her off her high horse and get her to be more cooperative.

Dominic's worried expression flitted from me to Dazielle. "Maybe you both need to take a break."

"Everything's under control," Dazielle said. "Return to your post, Dominic. Make sure no one gets in to that crime scene, especially not Tempest."

He turned to head back to the house and pulled up short.

"Is there a problem?" Dazielle asked.

Dominic ducked as Wiggles was ejected from the house like he'd been shot out of a rocket.

Wiggles rolled nose over tail several times before landing in a heap by my feet with a loud grunt.

He was swiftly followed by Bandit, who flew through the air, her paws outstretched. She latched on to the first thing she could find, which just happened to be Dominic's outstretched wing.

"Yow! Get those claws off me." Dominic shook his wing, but Bandit held on tight.

"Yum! So many delicious feathers to choose from." Bandit chomped on Dominic's wing, sinking her teeth through the downy mass.

Dominic yelped and continued to flap his wing as Bandit chewed on him.

Dazielle shook her head as she glared at me. "Does this creature have something to do with you?"

"Nope. I definitely don't own a cat," I said.

"You own that, though." She pointed to Wiggles, who was shaking out his fur and glaring over his shoulder at the house.

"The angels tossed us out," he grumbled. "One second, we were having a good poke around the body, and the next, we were flying through the air. Not particularly angelic behavior."

Dazielle hissed air through her teeth. "Your animals are messing up the crime scene."

"They're free spirits," I said. "I can't stop them from looking around if they want to."

"We got great information," Wiggles said. "It's definitely Viggo in there. He's very dead. Can't mistake that."

I glanced at Dazielle, whose face was turning an alarming shade of red. "How did he die?"

"Some sort of freaky magic," Wiggles said. "His face is petrified, like he literally died of fright. He's all frozen, and his hands are clawed up."

"That's enough," Dazielle muttered. "You've interfered with this investigation too much already."

Bandit was propelled away from Dominic as he finally got her free from his wing. She spun through the air with a yowl.

I reached up and grabbed her, instantly regretting it as claws sank into my skin. "Jeez! Let go."

Her wide eyes stared at me before she blinked and retracted her claws. "These angels are nasty. Although, their feathers sure are tasty." She had several small pieces of Dominic's feathers sticking out of her mouth.

"I'm happy you got a soft landing." I inspected the small red pin pricks on my skin as I set her on the ground.

"We saw the body," Bandit said.

"Tempest already knows that," Wiggles said. "I was filling her in on all the useful bits."

She sniffed. "Did you tell her how Viggo died?"

"Of course. This house must be where he was staying," Wiggles said.

"Is that true?" I asked Dazielle.

She pressed her lips together and shook her head.

"We're right," Bandit said. "There's an overnight bag in one of the bedrooms, and his things were in the bathroom. He was definitely staying here. His killer must have tracked him and got him when he was on his own."

"We don't know that for certain," Dazielle muttered.

"There are signs of a struggle too," Wiggles said. "Things were knocked over in the lounge, and there are scorch marks on the walls from magic spells."

"Any signs of a break-in?" I asked.

"We didn't get a chance to look," Wiggles said.

"Viggo wouldn't have let his attacker in unless he knew them. If there's evidence someone broke into the house, they could have been waiting inside for him to return," I said.

"Stop making assumptions." Dazielle scowled at me.

"They're not assumptions. They're well thought out theories based on evidence," I said.

"Provided by talking animals." Dazielle turned and stalked away. "Dominic, you're with me."

Dominic nursed his injured wing, a miserable look on his face as he turned to go.

I touched his arm. "Sorry about the cat attack."

"No problem." His nervous gaze went to Bandit before he vanished inside the house with Dazielle.

"How many angels are inside?" I asked Wiggles quietly.

"Four."

"Six in total if you count the ones out here," Bandit said. "Why?"

"Because, if most of the angels are at this crime scene, their headquarters will be almost empty. How about we get inside, see Raine, and get some answers out of her?"

"Sure, I'm up for anything," Wiggles said. "It'll be simple to get inside Angel Force undetected."

"You can't be trusted to get this right," Bandit said as we hurried away from the house.

"What do you mean, furball?" Wiggles bared his teeth.

"You got distracted by the trash when we were inside," Bandit said. "That's why the angels found us."

"Not true. I was investigating the garbage for clues when you knocked a pen off the counter. Why are you obsessed with knocking things on to the floor?"

Bandit ran along beside me. "It's an addiction. It doesn't matter what it is, a vase full of flowers, a mug of coffee, a pen. It's all the same. If it's on the table, it shouldn't be there. It doesn't feel right until I get it in its correct place."

"That's just weird," Wiggles said.

"It doesn't matter now," I said. "You both got useful information. Viggo was murdered by magic. I reckon someone is out to get rid of Magic Council members. We have to find out why."

I slowed as we reached the doors to Angel Force. "We need a distraction. There'll still be a few angels inside. Bandit, how cute can you look?"

She fluffed out her fur and curled her tail around her feet. Her pupils grew bigger and bigger until all I could see were enormous black, pitiful eyes blinking up at me.

"Aahh. That's so sweet," I said.

"I can be sweeter." Wiggles glared at me, ruffled his fur, and puffed out his cheeks. It looked like he was holding in gas.

I chuckled. "Bandit wins this one. Get in there and charm the angels. Make them think you need help and lead them outside. The second they come out, I'll go in and talk to Raine."

"What am I supposed to do?" Wiggles grumbled. "I should go in there."

"They know you. You've snuck in one too many times for them to trust you. Bandit's new to the village. It'll be easier for her to distract them without making them suspicious."

"That's the only reason, though," Wiggles said. "Otherwise, I'd be much better at doing this than her."

"Keep believing that, hound," Bandit said.

I petted his head. "Of course, you would. Now, go inside, Bandit, and be as cute as possible."

She slid a paw over one ear before nodding.

I eased the door open wide enough for her to get in and then hurried around the side of the building with Wiggles.

"She's failed," Wiggles said after we'd been waiting a few minutes. "Those angels won't believe she needs help. She's not even that cute."

"It had better work," I said. "I'm done with everyone hiding information. Raine needs to tell us what she knows."

He cocked his head. "You really think she's involved?"

"Yes, but I'm not sure how. This all leads back to the Magic Council. This murder isn't about a lover's tiff or Abigail's familiars. This is something much bigger."

"What's the plan when we go inside?"

"I'll go in alone. You stand guard by the door. Only come in to let me know if anybody is approaching."

"This isn't going to work. Bandit won't have—"

The door to Angel Force opened. Two angels walked out. One held Bandit like a baby, all four paws sticking up in the air.

"She's so pretty," the angel said. "Maybe she's lost. Do you need a new home, kitty cat?"

Bandit squirmed in the angel's arms and made a cute sounding chirrup.

"We should find her something to eat," the other angel said. "I wonder if she likes fish. Do you like fishies, cutie pie?" She tickled Bandit's exposed belly.

Bandit hopped out of the angel's arms and ran away a few steps before looking over her shoulder and giving a plaintive mew.

"Come back, kitty." The angels hurried after her.

Bandit hopped away and turned the corner, leading the angels out of sight.

"That's my cue," I said. "You wait here and be the lookout. I'll be as quick as I can." I hurried into the reception and was happy to see it empty.

I eased open the door and checked inside. I spotted an angel, but she was at the back of the office and turned away from me. It was the best chance I was getting.

I hurried through the office and into the cells.

Raine was the only occupant, and she jumped to her feet as she saw me. "Tempest! What are you doing here?"

"Looking for answers," I said. "Viggo Blowhard's just been murdered."

She took a step back. "What happened?"

"You knew he was here?"

"The angels told me. Who killed him?"

"That's what I'm trying to find out. But you need to be straight with me. What do you know about John Smith's death?"

Her gaze narrowed. "I've already told you I don't know the guy."

"You're lying. And I know you work for the Magic Council."

"How do you..." she sighed. "Was it Granny Dottie or Azura who told you?"

"Both. You, Viggo, and John are linked to the Magic Council, which means you know more than you're letting on. If you want out of here, you have to come clean. I want to help, but I can't do that if I only have half a story."

Raine slumped against the wall. "First off, I'm no murderer. I didn't kill John."

"I know that," I said. "But you're involved. How did you know John?"

She was silent for a long second. "He used to work at the Magic Council."

"You were in the same department?"

"Not as such. John worked in witness protection."

"Is that what you do?"

"No, my job is to monitor the activities of Magic Council employees and make sure they stay on the straight and narrow."

"And you were tracking John because you thought he was corrupt?" I asked.

She nodded. "I was certain of it. Working in witness protection is tricky, and staff are vulnerable to exploitation. They're always getting offers of bribes to share information and look the other way. They're looking after people with valuable information. It's the kind of information that'll put others away for a long time."

"John was looking after a witness when he came to Willow Tree Falls?"

She nodded again. "He's been on my radar for months. A witness he was supposed to protect disappeared in strange circumstances not so long ago. He pleaded innocence and said there was a leak in the department. He was lying, but I didn't have enough evidence to get him kicked out of the Magic Council. When I heard he got assigned this job, I took the case and followed him here."

"And that's why you got the sudden urge to come to the village," I said. "You're not here to see us; you were tracking John."

Raine shrugged. "Seeing you all was a bonus, but that's basically right."

"So, you confronted him about being corrupt on the night he died?"

"No, I didn't get that far," she said. "I didn't want him to know I was on to him, but I made a mistake. He caught me following him. We argued, and he told me to stay out of his business. He tried to pull rank and claimed he'd been in the Magic Council for over a decade and I didn't know what I was talking about. The thing is, I do. I always get a feeling about people as soon as I meet them. He had dodgy written all the way through him like poison."

"After you argued, what happened?"

"That was the last time I saw him," Raine said. "But I was worried. There were rumors he was involved with a dark magic user. No one knows who it is, but the witness he was supposed to protect had information against a group implicated in some dark affairs. That information could lock them away for a long time."

"And that's definitely worth killing for," I said.

"Exactly. I'm not sure what happened to John, though. Did he turn against the Magic Council, or did he change his mind? Maybe he grew a conscience and decided not to give up the location of the witness."

"And his dark magic contact killed him?"

"Possibly. Or a member of the dark magic group lost control around him, and his death was the unpleasant outcome. Whatever happened, John died as a result of his corruption. He was messing with powers too strong to control."

"Have you told this to the angels?" I asked. "They still think you're guilty."

She shook her head. "If I do, my hard work will have been for nothing. If I confess that I work at the Magic Council investigating corrupt employees, I'll have to resign. No one will trust me once they know. And the angels won't be able to keep this a secret."

"You're willing to risk going to prison to preserve your cover?" I couldn't decide if that was brave or foolish.

"It won't come to that," Raine said. "The angels don't have enough evidence to charge me. And despite what Dazielle thinks, it'll be a cold day in hell before I put my hands up to John's murder. They're leaving me here because they think I'll crack."

"Okay, I get the link to John, but what's your connection to Viggo?" I asked. "I'm guessing you know him too."

"I know his reputation," she said. "I was surprised when I learned he was in the village. Although, maybe it's not so odd. He specialized in tracking dark magic users. If John was meeting his dark magic contact, Viggo might have had a tipoff and come to investigate."

"He turned up to catch a dark magic user who wants the witness John was looking after and gets killed?"

"Most likely," Raine said. "The dark magic user murdered John, then when Viggo started poking around, he was gotten rid of as well."

"How important is this witness?" I asked.

"She's crucial," Raine said. "Simone has information that'll bring years of investigation to a close. She had her head turned by dark magic but changed when she fell in love."

"That's sickeningly sweet."

"Sweet but true. Her fiancé convinced her to tell the Magic Council what she knew. She did it on the condition she'd be put in protective custody along with her fiancé. The plan was to set them up in a new life when this was over."

"This witness is still out there, is that right?"

She nodded. "And while I'm stuck in here, she's vulnerable."

"Let me help," I said. "I can keep the witness safe. How hard can it be?"

"Have you forgotten the two bodies that just turned up in the village? Whoever it is, this dark magic user isn't messing around. If they find out you're involved in keeping the witness safe, there'll be a target on your back."

I shrugged. "I'm not worried about that. What kind of magic does Simone possess?"

"She's dark fey. Half-demon, half-fairy."

"Sounds powerful."

"Powerful but chaotic. Simone wasn't properly trained in her powers when she was young. They go off without warning. Don't forget that and expect to get a few glitter showers when you meet."

"Okay, avoid the glitter spurts. Where can I find her?"

Raine tilted her head back and groaned. "That's another problem. I have no idea."

Chapter 18

"You don't know where this witness is being kept?" I rubbed the back of my neck. This wouldn't be as easy as I'd first thought.

Raine approached the door of the cell. "That's the whole point of witness protection. The fewer people who know all the information about the witness, the better. It means, if there's someone corrupt on the inside, they don't have all the information they need to get to the witness or pass it on to someone who needs to silence them. Only John knew all the details of Simone's whereabouts. He set it up. All I know is she's somewhere in Willow Tree Falls."

"Where have you tried looking for her?"

"The hotel and all the rental properties. No luck in any of them," Raine said. "You have to find her, Tempest. She's vulnerable on her own. John's been dead for days, and she'll be panicked. For all I know, the dark magic user could have already gotten to her. Getting rid of Viggo might have been their way of tying up loose ends before they flee the village. We could already be too late."

"It's not a big place to search," I said, "but there are plenty of spaces to hide. I can start by asking around the stores. John would have been feeding Simone, so he must have brought supplies."

"It won't be long before Simone makes a move from wherever she's staying. If she's still alive and heads out alone, the dark magic user will find her. She won't stand a chance. She's young, untrained, and terrified."

"Come with me," I said. "You know this witness better than I do."

She shook her head. "I'm in a cell surrounded by magic."

"We just need to break through the barrier. The angels' magic isn't impenetrable." I hovered a hand close to the bars, and a warning pulse of something unpleasant made the hairs on my arms lift up and tingle.

"Don't think I haven't tried." Raine lifted her arms, and her sleeves dropped back to reveal shackles around her wrists. "The angels caught me trying to break through. These are magic drainers. I'm useless with these on."

I scowled. It would take me too long to break through the magic on my own. "Okay, sit tight. I'll start asking around about Simone. What does she look like?"

"She's short, less than five-foot-tall, shoulder-length black hair, and blue eyes. You'll know her when you find her because she literally sparks with energy. You'll probably be able to sense her before you see her as well. She has power, but it's not in her control."

"I'll do what I can," I said. "I have to get out of here. Most of the angels are busy investigating Viggo's murder, but they'll be back before long. If they find me talking to you, I'll be joining you in that cell."

"You need to hurry," she said. "This thing is about to blow up in our faces. If Simone vanishes, our case will fall apart."

I raised my eyebrows. "I'm only doing this because you're my cousin. This isn't to help the Magic Council."

She lifted a shoulder. "I know you don't love the Magic Council. I'm the same. That's why I joined, to change things. But I can't do that if I'm charged with murder."

"That's not going to happen." We said goodbye, and I hurried out of the cells, checking to make sure I wouldn't be seen as I legged it through the office and out to reception.

I'd just made it out the front door when the two angels returned, minus Bandit.

I nodded at them, trying to look innocent as I hurried away with Wiggles.

"So, what's going on?" he whispered.

I explained the situation with the missing witness and Raine's investigation. "We need to get hunting for this hidden magic user. We'll start at the stores and work our way through them. Somebody must have seen something that points us to Simone."

"I vote we start at Mystic Mushroom," Wiggles said. "Everyone who visits the village always tries the pizza. Tate's pizza making skills are legendary."

"And I'm guessing you're hungry?"

"I'm always hungry," he said. "And since that cat's gone, we don't need to worry about going somewhere that serves fruit."

I looked around. "Where is Bandit? She can't have gone far."

"Maybe she found a new home," Wiggles said. "Come on. I'm starving."

"Hey! Wait up," Bandit yelled.

Wiggles groaned. "Let's pretend we haven't heard her."

"Don't be mean," I said. "She helped us."

He growled and stomped ahead.

I turned and waited for Bandit. "Nice job back there."

"It was easy. Those angels sure are stupid. They fell for the kitten act in less than a minute. Big eyes, fluffed up fur, and plenty of pathetic squeaks, they were putty in my paws."

"You deserve a treat," I said. "We're getting pizza."

Her nose wrinkled. "I'll stick with the pineapple on the top."

"Fine by me. Although, Tate does a fruit pizza."

Bandit stopped dead and stared at me. "A pizza made entirely of fruit? It's like all my dreams come true."

I grinned. "The base is dough, but all the toppings are fruit. He uses maple syrup and strawberry jelly as the sauce. Can I interest you in a fruity pizza?"

Bandit curled around my legs and purred. "You're not so bad for a witch. I'm seriously considering making this my full-time gig."

"Not if Wiggles has anything to do with it."

She grumbled. "Dogs are too much responsibility. You should get rid of him and move me in. I'll be happy on my own for days with a huge fruit platter and a comfy cushion to snooze on."

"I'm not getting rid of Wiggles. Now, move it fluffball before my offer of fruit pizza vanishes."

She twirled around my legs one more time before striding ahead of me, her tail twitching.

We headed into Mystic Mushroom, and the delicious aroma of melting cheese, basil, and fresh dough filled my nose.

Tate was just returning to the counter when we arrived. He smiled when he saw us. "Hey, what will it be, Tempest?"

"Two extra cheese meat feast slices to go and a slice of fruit pizza."

Tate glanced at the cat. "Fruit pizza is off the menu today. I ran out of maple syrup."

Bandit's eyes narrowed.

"Have you got any fruit?" I asked.

"Pineapple," he said.

"I'll take a cup of pineapple."

His eyebrows rose. "Interesting order. Who's your new friend?"

"This is Bandit," I said.

"She's cute."

"You're not so bad yourself," Bandit said.

Tate's mouth opened before he laughed. "Trust you to get a talking cat."

"It's not what it looks like," I said. "I also need your help, as well as your delicious pizza. Did you serve John Smith, the guy who died in Abigail's store, at any point?"

Tate strolled behind the counter. "Sure. He came in twice, actually. The guy loved his pizza."

"What makes you say that?"

"He ordered a whole lot of food for just one guy. I even joked that he must be having a party, but he said it was all for him."

"Did you deliver any food to him?" I asked.

"Nope. He came in and got three boxes of pizza, two days in a row, though."

"Did you see where he went with his pizza?"

Tate's brow wrinkled. "He headed away from the stores, going toward the forest. I can't be certain because it was busy at the time. I'm pretty sure he took a right out of the door, though."

Which led to dozens of other places, including the forest.

"What's your interest in this guy?" Tate placed my order on the counter.

"You know me, always wanting to solve a puzzle."

He arched a brow. "And I heard your cousin's been locked up by the angels because of John's death. Is that why you're so keen on finding out what really happened to him?"

I shrugged as I handed over money and took our food. "Family first."

He grinned. "Always. Sorry I can't be any more help."

"You have been a help. Thanks." I hurried out with the food.

I passed Wiggles his pizza and dropped pieces of pineapple for Bandit to scoop up while I gave her a rundown on what Raine had told me.

"Where to now?" Wiggles asked.

"The forest," I said. "There are plenty of hiding places in there. John could easily have left Simone in a cave and told her to wait for him."

"Would she have waited this long?" Bandit asked. "If I was her, I'd be long gone by now. I wouldn't wait around for some guy to bring me more cold pizza."

"It's possible she's left her hiding place," I said. "If Simone's on the move in the forest, I know who we have to speak to."

"No way! I don't want to see Fallon." Wiggles stopped and glared at me.

"Who's Fallon?" Bandit asked.

"You know how you're a nightmare, and nobody likes you?" Wiggles asked.

"No, I don't know that," Bandit said.

"Well, Fallon is twice as bad," Wiggles said. "She's obsessed with riding me. She also sets lethal magic traps in the forest."

Bandit snorted a laugh. "You let her ride you?"

"No! Well, only in dire emergencies," Wiggles said.

"Fallon's the forest's guardian," I said to Bandit. "She's protective of her forest."

"No matter how many times I tell her, she keeps thinking I'm made to be ridden. She even had a saddle custom-made for me." Wiggles snorted. "Like I'm ever going to wear that."

"I bet you look cute in your saddle," Bandit said.

"You shouldn't sound so smug," he said. "I bet she'll want to ride you too."

Bandit hissed. "I'd like to see her try."

We headed into the forest and had been walking along the main path for five minutes, when there was a rustling above our heads, and Fallon appeared.

"Who goes there?"

"It's only us, Fallon," I called. "We're not about to walk into one of your magic traps, are we?"

"You never know your luck." She swung from the branch and landed in a crouched position before straightening. "Why are you in my forest?"

"We're looking for someone," I said.

"Who's this?" Fallon pointed at Bandit, her dark eyes gleaming with interest.

"A new friend," I said. "Bandit, meet Fallon."

"Hey," Bandit said.

"You have small ears." Fallon studied Bandit as she slowly walked around her.

"So do you," Bandit said. "Do you have a problem with creatures with small ears?"

"They're not so good for holding onto when you're being ridden. I'll need to get you a proper harness and a bit for your mouth, so you're easy to control."

"A what now?" Bandit stepped back.

Wiggles snorted a laugh. "I warned you."

"You're not as perfect as my little pony here." Fallon petted Wiggles' head. "His ears are ideal for holding onto when mounting him. It's just a shame his legs aren't a bit longer."

"You're not mounting me ever." Wiggles growled and stepped away.

"No one's mounting anybody," I said. "Fallon, we're looking for someone who's been in the forest for at least three days. She's called Simone. She's short, black hair, and blue eyes. She might have been brought in here by a tall guy wearing a suit."

"I've been here all that time," Fallon said. "I never leave my post. I even sleep with my eyes open. I've not seen anybody of that description in the forest."

"Are you absolutely certain?" I said. "She's at risk. Somebody wants to hurt her."

"I'd know if anyone was hiding in the forest," Fallon said. "What's she done?"

"Nothing bad," I said. "Have you heard about the murders in the village?"

"I've heard about one murder," Fallon said. "The guy in Abigail's store. There's been more?"

I nodded. "And I think they're connected to this missing person. Can you keep an eye out for her?"

"I can. In return, I'd like five rides on your pony, and I'll try a single ride on the fluffy donkey."

"No rides," Wiggles muttered.

"I'm not a donkey!" Bandit said. "Do you need your eyes tested?"

"You do have a strangely short snout for a donkey, but it's the fluff that gives you away. Donkeys always have that cute fluff on them," Fallon said. "I've got lots of carrots, fluffy donkey."

"I don't eat carrots." Bandit sniffed and looked away.

"Offer her a banana," Wiggles said.

"Quiet, hound," Bandit said.

"Fallon, focus!" I said. "It's important to watch out for this magic user. She's most likely scared and confused about what's going on. I don't want her getting hurt."

"If she walks into one of my traps, she'll very likely be hurt," Fallon said. "I'll let you know if I trap her."

"Thanks." Hardly reassuring, but it was the best offer I would get from Fallon. "We'll keep looking elsewhere."

We said our goodbyes, and Wiggles and Bandit raced out of the forest ahead of me. Neither of them seemed keen on being Fallon's new riding target.

I stopped at the edge of the forest when I spotted Mannie walking toward me.

He slowed and raised a hand. "Out for an afternoon stroll with your... pets?"

"No, I'm looking for somebody," I said. "Is Trixie not with you?"

Mannie shooed Wiggles and Bandit away as they sniffed around him. "I've got some business to attend to. She gets bored if I bring her with me."

"How's she doing after everything that happened in the store?" I asked.

"Still a little shocked, but I'm taking care of her. She's such a sweet young lady."

"Is it serious between you two?"

"It depends on your definition of serious." He ran a hand down his beard. "She's fun to be with, and we have a nice time together, but I'm not thinking of making her the next Mrs. Mannie Winter. Why do you ask?"

"Do you trust her?" I had promised I wouldn't mention her dalliance with John, but we were running out of time, and lives were in danger.

He spluttered a few words before puffing out his chest. "Of course."

"You're sure she was with you the night John died?"

His bushy eyebrows shot up. "I'm certain of it."

"You did say you'd had a lot to drink that night. Maybe you dozed off and don't remember everything."

His gaze went to the ground. "I was enjoying myself that night. I may have dozed occasionally but not for long. We had fun together and then went to bed. Why are you asking where she was?"

I sidestepped the question. "Has Trixie been acting strangely? Going out at odd times or anything like that?"

"Of course not. You don't think she's involved in what happened to John, do you? The angels have already talked to her about him. They're happy with her alibi." His eyes narrowed. "What do you know that they don't?"

"Nothing for certain," I said. "But my cousin's in the firing line for John's murder, and she's innocent."

"As is Trixie," Mannie said.

"She was definitely with you that whole night?" I leaned closer. "Mannie, as the mayor of this village, you need to keep your reputation intact. You don't want people hearing that you're covering for someone under scrutiny in a murder investigation."

More spluttering occurred as he scrubbed at his beard and frowned. "I did wake in the early hours, and Trixie wasn't in bed. I assumed she was in the bathroom. I didn't stay awake for many seconds and forgot all about it."

"Does she often get up in the middle of the night?"

His gaze grew anxious. "Tempest, you're worrying me. She's a good girl."

Which wasn't an answer. "Mannie, two people are dead."

"And Trixie isn't involved." He didn't sound all that convinced.

"I'm not saying she is, but what if she saw something that night and is too scared to say anything? The angels told me this involves dark magic. Anyone who witnessed something suspicious is at risk. You don't want Trixie getting hurt."

"Goodness, no! Of course not." He rolled the end of his beard around his fingers. "In truth, I have been a little concerned about her."

"Why is that?"

"Ever since Axel's sister came to town, she's been going out with her. They know each other from years ago but lost touch."

"Why is that a problem?"

He glanced over his shoulder. "There's something off about Foxglove."

"She's a half-demon," I said. "I get a bit twitchy around her too."

He shook his head. "It's more than that. I don't trust Foxglove. I'm worried she's leading Trixie astray. I overheard her telling Trixie I'm too old for her."

I pressed my lips together. The age gap between them was at least fifteen years. "Were they out together the night John died?"

"I can't confirm that," he said, "but Trixie's canceled on me twice since Foxglove's been in the village. Trixie drops everything to spend time with her."

"What are they doing?"

"That's another worrying thing," Mannie said. "Trixie doesn't like to talk about it. Although, she did mention Foxglove wanted a tour of the village."

"That's not so odd," I said.

"Trixie mentioned Foxglove is lonely. Axel keeps leaving her on her own, and she doesn't like that."

"Axel and Merrie are pretty serious. Maybe Foxglove was bored and thought she'd spend time with an old friend."

"Or she's looking for a man friend of her own and wants Trixie to find a new one as well and dump me." Worry crossed his face.

"I'm sure it's not that. Trixie's fond of you."

He grumbled under his breath for a few seconds. "Trixie also said Foxglove was interested in old buildings. Apparently, she's planning on buying something to renovate. She could be moving to Willow Tree Falls permanently if she finds something she likes. I'm not happy about that, not if she keeps telling Trixie to leave me."

My gaze narrowed. Foxglove didn't strike me as a property renovator type. "Did Trixie show Foxglove anything she liked?"

"She didn't say." He grabbed my arm. "Do you trust Foxglove? What if she persuades Trixie I'm not good enough for her?"

My mouth twisted to the side. "I don't know her all that well. She's always been friendly when we've met."

"Not to me, and now you're suggesting Trixie could be involved in this terrible business in the village. What if she's gotten in over her head? Foxglove could have set Trixie up with John and entangled her in his murder. My poor, innocent Trixie."

I resisted the urge to roll my eyes. She was definitely not innocent. "Maybe they're in on it together," I muttered more to myself than Mannie. "Could they be scoping out places to hide someone?"

He cocked his head. "Who would they want to hide? Do you think they're looking for a place to turn into a secret love nest?"

I shook my head. "I doubt it. Forget I said anything. And don't worry about Trixie. I think she'll be okay."

"I'm not so sure. I get the impression Foxglove's persuasive when she wants something. You don't think I have anything to worry about, do you?" Mannie asked. "She's a sweet young lady but not all that bright. I don't like to think of Foxglove using her."

"Where is Trixie today?" I asked. "I heard she's been missing work."

"That's another odd thing," he said. "She's normally reliable. Not since Foxglove turned up. She keeps missing appointments and forgetting things."

"You didn't whisk her away for some romantic adventure?"

His smile was a little smug. "Not recently. In fact, I've not seen her all day. Abigail's been in touch several times, asking where she is. I can't think what's gotten into her."

"Thanks, Mannie. I'm sure she'll turn up soon." Worry churned in my gut as I hurried away. What had Trixie gotten herself into, and what was her connection to Foxglove?

"You think they're working together?" Wiggles bounded along next to me, Bandit not far behind.

I shook my head. "I don't think Trixie knows what she's got herself into, but it sounds like Foxglove has been scoping out places that would be perfect for hiding Simone. What if she's looking for the hidden witness?"

"Huh! You think Foxglove's in Willow Tree Falls to kill this witness and keep her secrets quiet?" Wiggles asked.

I nodded. "She's a half-demon. Anything's possible. We need to find Foxglove and see what she's been up to."

Chapter 19

I jogged the short distance to Axel's bachelor pad and hammered my fist on the door.

Axel opened it a few seconds later. "Tempest and beasts! This is an unexpected pleasure. Are you—"

"No time for small talk. Where's Foxglove?" I peered over his shoulder.

"Oh! She's not here. Had you arranged to meet?"

"Where's she gone?"

"Not sure. She went out earlier today," he said. "Why don't you come in?"

I hurried inside and stood in the hallway. "Tell me where she was the night of John's murder."

Axel took a step back. "We were together all evening, hanging out. What's this about?"

"Where was she when Viggo Blowhard was killed? It happened about an hour ago."

"Viggo who?"

"He's from the Magic Council, investigating John's murder. Now he's dead too."

Axel frowned. "Bad luck, but I don't know anything about that. And the way you're talking, it makes me think you're blaming my sister for these murders."

"I won't if you can confirm she was with you on the night of John's murder," I said.

He glanced away and stuffed his hands into his pants pockets. "We were together."

"The whole time? She didn't leave at any point?"

"How about some coffee?" Axel turned and hurried into the kitchen.

I raced after him and grabbed his shoulder. "I don't want coffee. I want answers. There are more lives at risk. Someone in Willow Tree Falls is killing people to hide a dark secret."

He glared at me. "Foxglove might walk a dark line now and again, but that's in her nature. It doesn't make her a bad person."

"Tell me where she is. I can ask her all about that dark line."

He tugged on his bottom lip. "I'm not her keeper. She's free to come and go as she likes."

"And has she been doing that a lot since she arrived?"

Concern crossed Axel's face. "Maybe. Foxglove's a busy woman. I don't keep tabs on her every movement."

"I'm not interested in her every movement, but I would like to know if she was with you that evening," I said. "I know she's family but don't cover for her if she's up to something bad."

His fingers flexed, and he turned to the counter in the kitchen. "What does it matter if she went out for about an hour?"

"To do what?"

He glanced at me. "Nothing dodgy. She simply said she was meeting a friend."

"And where did they meet? Who is this friend?"

"I don't remember. She didn't tell me. Let's have a coffee. This has nothing to do with Foxglove. She's here visiting me; that's all."

"What's she been doing while she's been here?" I asked.

"Not much. We've had lunch together a few times. She's taken a few walks. Nothing exciting."

"Has she been looking for somewhere to live?"

His eyes widened. "No! I mean, I don't think so. If she has, she's not mentioned it to me. Foxglove already has her own place."

"But she's doing something that involves looking at old houses?"

He shrugged. "That's nothing. She's got a thing for old buildings. Foxglove's into visiting creepy places."

"And how does she know about all the creepy places in Willow Tree Falls?" I asked. "Have you been showing her?"

"No. She went out with Trixie a couple of times," Axel said. "She was showing her anything she considered spooky. Foxglove loves anything like that."

"And you don't think that's weird?" I asked.

"It's not weird at all. It's a hobby."

Wiggles nudged me with his nose. "What's the spookiest place in Willow Tree Falls?"

"Your dog bed?" Bandit said.

I sucked in a breath as my stomach flipped over. "Castle Fall ruins."

Wiggles nodded. "It's the perfect hideout. Most people are too terrified to step into that place.

You could easily hide someone there because you'd know nobody else would dare go in."

"Has Foxglove said anything about visiting the castle ruins?" I asked Axel.

"What she does in her spare time is her business," he said. "I don't like where you're going with this, Tempest."

"I'm going along the path of clearing my cousin's name and finding out who murdered John Smith and Viggo Blowhard."

"Then you're looking in the wrong place if you think it was Foxglove," he said.

"You just admitted you covered for her on the night of John's murder," I said.

"I wasn't covering anything," he said. "She just had to go out for an hour. There's no crime in that."

"There is if her visit included killing John and concealing his body in Abigail's store."

"That's not her style," Axel said. "Sure, my family has a dark side. We are half-demons, after all. But you can see by my shining example that we don't always turn to the dark side. Foxglove is the same as me."

"Has Foxglove started working with your dad yet?"

His gaze narrowed. "I believe so. That means nothing. Lots of people work for him."

True enough, but Kroni was a hard-core, scary demon. You had to pick up a few dark desires from rubbing shoulders with him. "When was the last time you saw her?"

"This morning," he said. "She told me she was heading out for the day and not to wait up."

"Let me guess. She didn't tell you where she was going or who she was planning to see, right?"

He sucked in a breath. "Correct. And there's nothing wrong with that."

"Thanks, Axel." I turned and headed toward the front door.

He raced after me and grabbed my elbow. "Tempest, don't do anything foolish."

"Like stop the killer?" I shook off his hand.

He grimaced. "I'll admit Foxglove's a little darker than I am. She uses her demon ability more frequently, and that makes her strong."

"Does that darker side involve killing people?"

"No! I mean, I don't think so. And she wouldn't do that here. She would only kill to defend herself or her family."

"Maybe that's exactly what she's doing."

His head lowered for a second. "Be careful if you confront her. She doesn't take kindly to being accused of something she hasn't done."

"I can handle her. I have my own ability plus a backup demon if things get difficult."

"And she has me," Wiggles said.

"And me," Bandit said.

I nodded. "Exactly. All I want to do is talk to her. Maybe this is a mistake, and she isn't involved. But Foxglove did turn up around the same time two people got murdered, and you can't tell me where she was at the time of John's murder. It doesn't look great."

He ran a hand down his face. "She didn't kill those guys, though. You'll see. And I'll want an apology for putting my sister in the frame for these murders."

"I'll be happy to give you one if she's really innocent." I pulled open the front door and walked out with Wiggles and Bandit. I glanced over my shoulder as we hurried away.

Axel was watching us, concern on his face.

I couldn't worry about hurting his feelings right now. We were about to go to the creepiest place in Willow Tree Falls and see if Foxglove was lurking in the shadows, looking for Simone. That had to be my focus.

"What's so epically scary about this castle?" Bandit ran along beside me.

"Have you ever watched the movie *Dracula*?" Wiggles asked.

"Of course," Bandit said.

"Remember the place he stayed in Transylvania? Super creepy, big turrets, lots of stone, freezing cold, succubi in the basement, evil shadows everywhere?"

"Which version of the movie did you see?"

"The best one," Wiggles said. "Anyway, Castle Falls is ten times worse than that. The last owner moved out almost fifty years ago. It's been sold several times since then, but the new owners never stay more than a couple of months."

I nodded. "The last person who tried ran screaming from the castle and hasn't been the same since. He claimed something got into bed with him, and he can still feel their icy fingers tracing over his body. Add in the regular appearances of ghosts with severed heads, furniture that moves on its own, and things that scream in the middle of the night, and it's a pretty unpleasant place."

"There was also a fire there not so long ago," Wiggles said. "People blame the unhappy spirits who still live there. They want to make sure nobody ever moves into their home, so they made it uninhabitable. The turrets were destroyed in the fire, and most of the rooms are unsafe."

"It still doesn't stop a few people from going inside on a ghost hunt," I said.

"And when they do, they come out changed," Wiggles said. "They see things that will turn your fur white."

"And we're really going in there?" Bandit asked.

"You're welcome to stay behind," Wiggles said, "if you're too scared to come with us."

She growled at him. "I'm scared of nothing. Ghosts don't bother me."

Castle Falls sat on the top of a hill, overlooking the whole village. It was set away from the forest and all the houses, giving a great view if you ever dared to climb the hill to the castle.

I was panting as I reached the top, and paused for a moment, resting my hands on my knees as I sucked in deep breaths. I needed to do more cardio.

I peered up at the busted windows. "If John was crazy enough to go inside, this is the perfect hiding place for Simone."

"Would Trixie have brought Foxglove here?" Wiggles asked. "She's not the bravest of women."

"It's hard to miss a castle," I said. "Even if Trixie didn't bring her here, Foxglove would have checked it out."

"So, we've found the killer," Bandit said.

"Not yet," I said. "I don't want to assume it was her, but her demon side could have taken over, especially now she's working with her dad. Kroni doesn't go around handing out puppies. His work involves darkness."

"And Simone got to know Foxglove when she started using dark magic," Wiggles said.

"Until she changed her mind," I said. "Foxglove could have figured out what was going on, used her inside link with John, and then killed him and Viggo."

"Now she's after Simone," Bandit said. "What powers does Simone have?"

"She's not short on power, being a half-demon, but according to Raine, she's never been trained. She won't be able to defend herself. On her own, she's vulnerable. Foxglove will exploit that."

My pulse was no longer racing as I strode to the broken wooden door to the castle. I peered into the gloom. The shadows looked dense and less than welcoming.

"Who's going first?" Wiggles asked.

"We'll go in together," I said. "And keep quiet. We need to listen for signs of anyone in here. It's a big place, and John could have hidden Simone anywhere."

"She could be hiding from us," Wiggles whispered. "Maybe she realized she's at risk, especially when John didn't return. She's holed up somewhere, keeping away from Foxglove."

"Let's hope she found a good hiding place." Taking a deep breath, I stepped over the threshold and looked around.

The stone entranceway was blackened with soot, and large pieces of burned wood lay on the floor.

I stepped over them and passed charred tapestries on the walls, the temperature plummeting by at least ten degrees as we moved farther into the castle.

I jumped as a pigeon shot from the rafters and flew out of an opening. I rolled my shoulders and kept inching forward.

The first room we came to looked to be an abandoned dining hall. An enormous stone fireplace was set at one end, and there were several old benches overturned and blackened with smoke.

I crept around the space, but there was nowhere obvious to hide. I gasped as tiny daggers pierced through my calf.

Bandit had attached herself to my leg and was clinging on, her eyes wide and fur puffed out.

"What's the matter with you?" I eased her claws out of my flesh.

"I'm getting a bad feeling about this place," she said. "There has been a lot of misery here. I feel it oozing from the stone like an infected wound."

I detached her from my leg and rubbed the skin through my jeans. "Let's keep looking."

The next room had a few pieces of furniture, suggesting it might have been a sitting room a long time ago. There was nothing useful in there.

We looked in the kitchen, an enormous walk-in pantry, and the sad remnants of what must once have been an incredible library but now contained moldy books and sagging shelves.

We all jumped as something metallic clanged behind us.

I turned and walked cautiously back along the main hallway.

Bandit hugged close to my ankles. "What was that?"

"That's what I'm trying to find out," I muttered.

"Probably rats," Wiggles said. "Bound to be giant rats living here. I bet they're the size of me. Maybe bigger. They'd easily take down a small furball like you. You'd make a nice snack for a hungry rat."

Bandit simply hugged closer to my ankles. Her lack of a snarky comeback showed her nerves.

The clanging came again. I stopped and stared at a tarnished suit of armor that stood at the bottom of the stairs. My eyes widened as one of the arms slowly lifted, a finger pointing up the stone staircase.

"Why is it doing that?" Bandit's voice wavered. "That's not normal."

"Maybe he's showing us where to find Simone?" I whispered.

"Or pointing to our certain doom," Bandit said. "We should leave."

"I thought you weren't scared," Wiggles said.

"Are you telling me you're not scared of a suit of armor that moves on its own?" Bandit said.

"There's nothing in the armor," Wiggles said. "It's just a ghost."

"Just. A. Ghost?" Bandit shook her head.

The visor of the suit of armor lifted. Two red eyes stared out at us before the finger waggled at the staircase.

I quickly shuffled past and dashed up the stone steps with Wiggles and Bandit. "Let's not debate this in front of the spooky suit of armor. We'll find out where it's sending us soon enough."

The stairs were littered with broken pieces of wood and fragments of burned tapestries. Several oil paintings hung crookedly on the walls as we hurried past them.

We rounded the corner of the staircase, and I stopped dead. At the very top of the stairs was a huge floating woman with long red hair and black eyes.

I cleared my throat. "Hi. I hope you don't mind the intrusion. We're looking for someone."

The ghost floated in the air, turning as she did so. She folded her hands in front of her and tilted her head as if waiting for me to continue.

I took a couple of steps closer. Bandit wrapped herself around my leg again and refused to budge. Even Wiggles kept close to my side.

"I don't know if you've seen her. She's probably been here a few days. Her name's Simone. She's short, black hair, and she's in trouble."

The ghost lifted a finger to her lips and pressed it against them softly.

"Is that a no you haven't seen her, or you don't want to talk about it?"

"Maybe she's telling you to keep quiet?" Bandit whispered.

"She could help us find Simone," I muttered. "She must be a resident, so she sees what's going on in this place."

The ghost drifted higher, not seeming interested in wanting to chat.

I shrugged. "Fair enough. Is it okay if we get past?" I drew nearer to the ghost.

She bared her teeth, looking nothing like the sweet human ghost she'd just been. Her black eyes flared, and her fingers extended to look like claws. She tripled in size before she launched toward us.

A cold blast smashed me in the chest, and I was suddenly flying down the stairs. I threw my hands out and grabbed the tattered remnants of a tapestry. I swung in the air for a second before pitching back toward the stairs. I landed on my hands and knees. Bandit was still attached to my leg.

The ghost gave an ear-splitting shriek as she rushed down the rest of the stairs and vanished through the stone wall.

I sucked in a breath and patted myself down gently. Everything was intact, although my leg was covered in deep scratch marks from where Bandit had clung.

I turned slowly to see Wiggles hadn't fared so well. He was halfway down the stairs, flat on his back, his legs poking in the air.

"Everything okay back there?" I staggered down the stairs to Wiggles, not aided by Bandit still clinging to me like a vicious limpet.

"I've been turned to ice," Wiggles said. "That ghost slammed straight into me."

I rolled him carefully to his feet and briskly rubbed him from head to toe to help him get warm.

He gave a big shiver before blasting out a small fireball and setting light to several pieces of wood. He raced over and sat right by them.

"We really need to leave," Bandit whispered. "I have a terrible feeling about this place. We are all going to die."

"We've only searched the ground floor," I said. "Once we get past the angry ghosts, we'll be fine."

"What if we don't get past the next angry ghost?" Bandit said. "What if that one throws us through a window?"

I glanced up the stairs. The mean ghost at the top had vanished for now. "Come on. We need to keep looking." I yanked a reluctant Bandit off my leg, and after a minute of warming ourselves on Wiggles' fire, we headed to the top of the staircase.

I'd only gone a few steps to my right before there was a sob.

"This way." I beckoned Bandit and Wiggles to follow. I eased open a door, which gave an ominous creak, like it hadn't been opened in a long time.

Sitting in a chair at the back of the room was Trixie. She was bound with a gag covering her mouth and tears streaking down her cheeks.

I raced over to her and pulled off the gag. "What's going on? Why are you here?"

Her whole body shook, and fresh tears spilled onto her cheeks. "She's terrible. Had no idea. She's a bad person."

"Slow down. Who are you talking about?"

"Foxglove. She's evil."

Worry punched into me as my fears about Foxglove were confirmed. "She tied you up here?"

Trixie nodded. "She lied. Said she wanted a home. She had to look here. I told her no. I told her the stories of the castle, but she insisted. Spent ages poking in corners as if looking for something. I asked what she was doing, but she got angry. Then she got mean." A sob shot out of her lips. "She left me here. Thought I would die. My Mannie must be scared."

"Calm down," I said. "I'll get you out of here. Do you know if Foxglove found what she was looking for?" I tried to loosen the bindings on Trixie's wrists, but the rope was dug in tight, and it stung as I touched it. It was covered in a dark magic spell.

"She didn't say," Trixie said. "Before we came here, she look at several other buildings, all old and abandoned like castle. I told her there were nicer houses, but she wanted a doer upper. Then come here and her eyes light up, as if she'd found perfect home. This is perfect home if you no have sound mind. There's something wrong with Foxglove."

"You're not the only one who thinks that," I said. "I can't get these bindings loose on your arms." I froze as a creaking floorboard moved behind me.

I spun around, but there was no one there.

My stomach flipped as the room grew hot and sparked a spell on my fingers.

Wiggles growled. "My gut's telling me something else is here."

"Another ghost?" Bandit inched toward me.

I raised my hand to fire a blast spell at the sound of another creak.

The room was plunged into darkness. Trixie whimpered, and Wiggles growled again.

I gasped in pain as I was flipped off my feet by the blow on the side of my head.

Then I was falling, falling, falling. All I could feel were Bandit's claws in my leg. Then nothing.

Chapter 20

My gritty feeling eyes slowly opened. I blinked several times as my vision came into focus. My head pounded, my mouth tasted like I'd licked the bottom of a hamster cage, and my arms burned. I tried to move them, but they were tightly tied behind my back, and the rope holding me tingled with dark energy.

I slowly moved my head from side to side. Nothing felt broken, but I had a painful lump on the left side of my head.

"Tempest!" Wiggles hissed. "Wake up. I've been trying to get you to open your eyes for ages."

"I'm awake," I mumbled. "What happened?"

"She happened," he said.

I lifted my head, the throbbing ache intensifying. Standing in the middle of the room was Foxglove, a scowl on her face.

I groaned. "We were right. This is all your doing."

She walked over and nudged me with her boot. "Clever you. My brother warned me you were nosy. I should have kept out of your way."

I sucked in a breath and slowly eased myself into a seated position. Trixie still sat tied to the chair, a terrified look in her eyes. Wiggles and Bandit had also been tied together. The scowl on their faces told me exactly how they felt about that. And, sitting on the edge of a moldy looking bed was a short woman with jet black hair, big round eyes, and a shimmer of what looked like glitter surrounding her. That must be Simone.

I shuffled back until I hit the wall to give myself some support. "How did you think you'd get away with this, Foxglove? You turn up and people start dying."

She shrugged. "It's not my first visit to the village. My brother lives here. Why is it so strange that I'm here as these unfortunate events unfold? Besides, two of your family members arrived just before bodies started dropping, and the angels are much more interested in your cousin than me. I'm happy for them to keep pursuing that line of inquiry. While they do so, I'll tidy up my loose ends and get out of here."

"No, you won't." I dropped the barriers inside me, and Frank's energy shot up my back and warmed me from the inside out.

Foxglove waggled a finger in the air. "You keep your tricks to yourself. You've got too much to lose if you let your demon loose."

I bared my teeth. "I'm not afraid to go up against you."

She strode over and grabbed Wiggles around the throat, hauling him and Bandit up with one hand. She was strong.

Wiggles kicked his feet in the air and flames flickered from his lips.

"You be on your best behavior too, doggy," Foxglove said. "If Tempest tries anything against me, I'll end your foul-smelling existence. And if you try anything to save her, I won't hesitate in killing Tempest."

I growled at the same time as Wiggles. "Leave him alone."

"What about me?" Bandit gasped. "Doesn't anybody care about me?"

"I have no idea what you are," Foxglove said. "You reek of fairy, but you look like a cat. Since you're here, you're not getting away. I can't have anybody knowing what I've done."

"Then you have a problem. People do know what you've done." I kept my attention on Wiggles and Bandit. "Before I came here, I spoke to Axel. He also has doubts about you. You're not going to kill your brother to make sure no one suspects you."

Her bottom lip jutted out. "He's my half-brother. And he's an embarrassment to the family. Even after spending time with our father and getting stern reminders as to his role in this community, he's lost his way once again."

"Axel's never lost his way," I said. "He's a decent guy, most of the time."

"Exactly my point. He's always preferred to be a decent guy rather than face his true responsibilities. And since he's fallen in love, he's grown weak. As soon as I saw him with that bartender, I realized he was lost to the family."

"You want to disown Axel because he's happy?"

"Disowning him will make it easier for me to get rid of him," she said. "I have a bigger mission than trying to keep my estranged family happy. If Axel becomes a problem, he dies."

"I get that you run with a darker crowd than most of us, but there's still good in you. I see that when you're with Axel. Despite what you've said, you like him. You won't kill him."

She snorted a laugh. "Like Axel? My weak half-sibling is a humiliation. I'll have to report back to Father what I've seen in my time here. He was grooming Axel for greater things. In a few years, he might have been ready to take over some of the family business, but now? Walking around with some sappy smile on his face and telling me he's never felt happier than when he's with Merrie. We don't do that. We don't fall in love. We don't become entangled in weak emotions that prevent us from fulfilling our destinies."

"And what's your destiny?" I asked. Frank lurked in the background, eager to get out and see what was going on. I longed to let him loose, but the way Foxglove had hold of Wiggles' neck, I couldn't risk it. He was pretty hard to kill, but in the hands of a half-demon, he was vulnerable.

"Foxglove's part of a dark magic syndicate." Simone glanced at me. She had dark shadows under her eyes, and it looked like her hair hadn't been washed for days.

"A syndicate? What do they plan to do?" I asked.

"Bring down the Magic Council," Simone said.

"That's enough from you," Foxglove snapped. "If you hadn't betrayed our friendship, I wouldn't be here. The deaths of those two men are on your hands. You should have kept your mouth shut and not grown afraid of what we had planned, then none of this would have happened, and you wouldn't be about to die."

"How do you plan to bring down the Magic Council?" I asked.

"By bringing dark power to the fore," Foxglove said. "Things haven't always been this way. It hasn't always been the ridiculous, stuffy rules of the Magic Council preventing people from using their true abilities. Demons once had a lot more control."

"You mean, things were out of control. You didn't stick to the designated magic zones. You strayed into human territory and injured people who had no clue we even exist."

"It's hardly our fault humans lack any ability to defend themselves," Foxglove said. "And why shouldn't we have full control? We're more powerful. There may be many more humans than us, but we have strength they can only dream of. Actually, we're a part of their worst nightmares. They know we exist but deny it because it fills them with fear. How is it right that we have to stay in certain zones and keep ourselves secret? It's not. I'm not the only one who's grown tired of the Magic Council restricting us. Powers range from light to dark. It's a part of nature. Why hold us back when we're doing nothing wrong?"

"I call killing people wrong," I said.

Trixie sniffled and shifted in her seat. "I have nothing to do with this. Please, let me go. Won't tell anybody what I know. Love my life here. Happy with Mannie."

"So happy, you sucked face with John." Foxglove smirked. "You got yourself into this mess. You played around, and now you're paying the price. Mannie won't want you when you get charged with double murder."

My eyes widened. "You're setting Trixie up to take the fall for this?"

"Don't sound so surprised. You thought the same thing," Foxglove said. "You wondered if Trixie had killed John. A spurned lover seeking revenge is a plausible motive for murder."

"My suspicions were only helped by you," I said. "You lied to me. You told me you saw Trixie and John together."

"It wasn't a lie," Foxglove said. "They were together that evening. I can hardly blame her. The guy she's with is never going to make super stud of the year."

"Might not be handsome man, but he good to me," Trixie said. "I made mistake."

"Your mistake played into my hands," Foxglove said. "And given the fact you've been sneaking around with me makes you look even more suspicious. Your behavior's out of character. That's going to get noticed." She turned to me and grinned. "Although, arranging for a witch who carries a demon inside her to be responsible for the murders might be even more fun. Could I get away with setting that up, I wonder?"

My eyebrows shot up. "No way! There's no chance you're pinning these murders on me."

She tilted her head from side to side. "I don't know. Everybody's aware there's a dark streak running through you. I sense it now. Your demon's desperate to get out and wreak havoc. The trouble is, when he does, you won't be able to control him. Perhaps you lost control when you confronted John and Viggo. Your demon came out to play, and you wound up with two dead bodies on your hands."

"It doesn't work like that," I growled out. Although, it sort of did. When Frank was in full control, it was almost impossible to stop him.

She chuckled. "Oh, yes. We're going to have a lot of fun with your demon. Perhaps, I can call him to me. We are of the same dark family. He'd be willing to be on my side and enjoy himself while I sit back and watch my problems vanish in a haze of violence."

"Frank's not coming out." Even as I said those words, his power inched over my head. Did he want to come out and meet Foxglove? Would he consider her an ally?

"Let him loose for me to control, or the hellhound gets it." Foxglove shook Wiggles.

His eyes bugged, and he kicked out at her.

"It's not happening," I said.

"It is. And you're going to start with Simone. You need to kill her. All evidence of my involvement has to be wiped out."

Simone whimpered, and her gaze shot to me. A spark of glittery magic slid from her palm.

I shook my head. "I won't do it."

"It's your choice. You either kill Simone or I kill this mutt and then the cat. What will it be?" Foxglove asked.

I swallowed, my mouth dry as I looked around for a way to escape.

A blast of energy shot from Simone and headed toward Foxglove. She spun around and held Wiggles and Bandit in front of her. They received the full blast of magic and were covered in a glittery explosion of light.

"Stop! Don't do that." I glared at Simone. "You don't have control of your ability. You'll injure someone."

She ducked her head. "I'm trying to help."

"Pathetic." Foxglove dropped Wiggles and Bandit to the floor. They flailed around, their legs spasming as the magic ran through their bodies.

I looked over to see if Trixie could help, but her shoulders were slumped and her head down. She looked defeated.

Foxglove stood in front of Wiggles and Bandit, her hands splayed, ready to blast them with more magic. "I'll ask you one last time, Tempest. Who do you value more? Kill a stranger and keep these creatures you seem so attached to, or sacrifice them to protect the Magic Council? You're not a fan of the Council. They've hounded you and your family for years. Why sacrifice what you care about for them? They won't thank you. They might even blame you for this mess. You need to do the right thing and think of yourself. Destroy Simone and you may have your hellhound and your cat back."

I gritted my teeth. Magic flared through my fingers, trying to eat away the bindings, but strong dark magic held them in place.

Foxglove shook her head. "You fool. You pick an organization that has done nothing for you. So be it. Say goodbye to your hellhound."

I sucked in a breath, my heart racing.

The door behind Foxglove slammed open. Axel stood there, horror filling his eyes as he took in the scene. "Foxglove, what are you doing?" He took a step into the room.

She spun on her heel. "This is no place for you, brother."

"What are you doing here?" I asked him.

"I followed you." He took another step. "Foxglove, why have you got Tempest tied up? And Trixie? What's this about? I didn't believe Tempest when she said you could be involved with killing John and Viggo, but this looks... weird."

"Walk away," Foxglove growled out. "Leave now and you don't have to be involved."

He swallowed loudly before shaking his head. "I can't do that. Tell me what you're doing. Did you really kill those guys?"

My gaze shifted as Wiggles rolled to his feet. Foxglove had strapped Bandit to Wiggles' back, so her feet now pointed at the ceiling. Wiggles shook himself and looked at me.

My stomach flipped as his red eyes flared with rage. He was planning something. I didn't want Wiggles and Bandit in the middle of this fight. It was about to get messy.

Axel moved even closer to his sister, his hands held out. "Whatever you're involved in, we can fix it."

"I don't want to fix it," Foxglove said. "This is what I'd planned to do all along."

"Kill John and Viggo?" he asked.

She shrugged a shoulder. "Viggo was a bonus. That irritating official has been on my back for too long. He got a tipoff I was here and came poking around. It was the excuse I needed to get rid of him. I always planned to kill John. He's a cheating liar. He promised to hand Simone over then went back on his deal. If only he'd stuck to his word and given her to me, he'd still be alive."

Axel scraped a hand through his hair, disappointment shimmering in his eyes. "What's made you turn so dark?"

"Nothing's made me turn," she snapped. "This is me. This is what we are. We're a part of the same family, but you've always been too afraid to face your destiny."

"Our destiny isn't to turn into killers."

She snorted a laugh. "All you care about is making nice with Merrie. All that talk about marriage, happy families, and settling down. It's humiliating. You want to marry a witch. What's the matter with you?"

"The matter with me?" Axel scowled at her. "You've just admitted to killing two people."

I looked back at Wiggles. His butt was wriggling and his muscles bunched. I couldn't risk telling him not to move. It would alert Foxglove.

I bit my bottom lip, my heart pounding as he launched onto Foxglove's back.

She shrieked and slammed to the floor as Wiggles bounced on top of her, and Bandit hissed and spat her fury, her little legs kicking in the air.

"Move! Now!" he yelled at me.

I rolled to my side and used the wall to get to my feet. It was time to make this half-demon pay.

Chapter 21

The dark magic binding my wrists burned my skin as I fought against it.

"Simone, can you deal with this?" I hurried over to her, keeping a close eye on Foxglove, who was still battling Wiggles and Bandit. I only had a few seconds.

Her eyes widened, and she shook her head. "I don't want to hurt you with my magic."

"I have to get free of these bindings." My gaze was fixed on Wiggles, whose jaw was clamped around Foxglove's shoulder. Any second now, she'd get free and go gunning for him.

"No! My magic isn't stable." Simone said.

"Please! We don't have time." I raised my hands behind me. "You have to burn through this magic, or we all die."

She swallowed. "Okay. Just be really still. Don't move a muscle."

My gut tightened as a hot swell of magic pulsed across my hands and up my arms. A second later, a cascade of glitter poured over me.

I blinked glitter out of my eyes. "Were the sparkles necessary?" It fell from my hair as I shook my head, releasing about a pound of glitter onto the floor.

"It happens when I'm nervous." More glitter poofed from Simone.

I rubbed my stinging wrists and looked over at Axel. His face was torn with conflict. I didn't blame him. His sister was trying to take everyone down. Who would he pick, his friends or his family? I couldn't rely on him as backup in this fight.

"Can you move?" I asked Simone.

She shook her head. "Foxglove's put a draining spell on me. I can barely stand. All I want to do is sleep."

"Then keep your head down and stay out of this." Glitter fell off my arm as I patted her shoulder.

A yelp had me spinning. Wiggles had been tossed away by Foxglove, but he was still tied to Bandit. She was firmly attached to Foxglove's thigh, her teeth sunk through the fabric of her pants and her claws deeply embedded.

Foxglove snarled and swiped at Bandit.

Wiggles was hanging upside down, his legs flailing in the air as he burped fire and yelled rude words.

Foxglove reached around, caught Wiggles by the collar, and ripped Bandit off her leg. She hissed in her face. "You're going to pay for that." She tossed them in the air and raised a hand, a jagged ball of something sticky and dark forming on her palm.

I blasted her with a knockback spell before racing forward and catching Wiggles and Bandit as they tumbled through the air.

Their combined weight sent me to my knees, but I softened their fall. They tumbled out of my arms and lay panting on the floor.

I sliced through their bindings with my own magic. "Get out of here, you two. Get Trixie and Simone free and leave."

"I'm not leaving you alone with that crazy demon," Wiggles said.

I ushered them away. "There's no time to debate this. Get the others out of here. I'll handle Foxglove."

She was already climbing to her feet, sparks of red and black magic flickering across her skin and an expression of pure hatred etched on her face.

"Go! Get the others out of here." I pushed Wiggles toward Trixie and Bandit toward Simone.

"You're going to deal with me?" Foxglove almost growled as she spoke. "You'll be dead in seconds."

"I wouldn't bet on that," I sneered. "No one threatens my hellhound and lives to tell the tale."

"Foxglove, you have to stop," Axel said.

Her harsh glare flicked to him. "Whose side are you on, brother? Are you considering supporting this witch over your family?"

I shook my head at him. I didn't want him to have to make that choice. What if he chose his sister, and I had to go up against them both? "Axel, you don't need to be involved."

"But I am." Disappointment haunted his voice. "This is wrong."

I glanced over to see Wiggles helping Trixie out of her restraints, while Bandit was nudging Simone slowly toward the door.

I stalked around Foxglove, forcing her attention back to me, so she couldn't see what they were doing. "Give yourself up and the angels might go easy on you."

"Of course, they will. After all, angels are such good friends with demons. No, this ends now. You end now." She slammed a spell at me.

I ducked out of the way as it skimmed over my head.

Several more foul-feeling spells slammed toward me as I ducked and hustled my way around the room, not wanting to experience the weird blend of dark demon power she used. Foxglove was shooting to kill.

I snarled at her. I had tricks of my own if she intended to play dirty, and one of them was called Frank. Now that the risk to the others was minimized, I finally let him out.

It felt like he gave a long stretch as I released him, starting from my toes and creeping up my legs, over my chest, and seeping through my hair, making the follicles warm.

"Ready when you are," I muttered.

"What have we here?" Frank muttered. "Demons, demons, and more demons. You have been busy."

"You know what's going on," I said. "Do you want to get involved or just keep flapping your lips?"

Foxglove's eyes narrowed. "Your demon can't help you. I'll bring this place down on our heads if I have to. No one's getting out alive."

That's where she was wrong. Everyone was getting out, although I might make an exception for her.

"What kind of demon have you got living inside you?" Foxglove cocked her head. "He can't be that powerful if you've had him contained all these years."

"You hear that, Frank? Foxglove doesn't think you're up to much," I said.

He growled in my head. "You'd be surprised how powerful I am."

My voice lowered an octave as Frank took over, and my body felt like it had been lit on fire.

Foxglove slammed me with her demon magic. With Frank in control of my movements, I had to endure the impact. I wished he'd remember how fragile my body was. Demons could survive multiple magic strikes, thanks to their tougher skin. Witches, not so much.

She screamed and raced forward, her hands outstretched. Her hatred washed over me as her fingers curled into my hair and smashed me into the wall.

"I will kill you," she hissed in my face.

"Not if I get you first." Frank's energy ripped through me, and his power doubled my strength.

Foxglove flew backward and hit the floor, giving a startled grunt as she landed.

I grabbed her and held her down, my hands wrapping around her throat. I had her. She was on her knees in front of me and couldn't move.

"Tempest, don't kill her," Axel said. "What she's done is wrong, but she's still my sister. We can take her to the angels. They'll punish her."

I didn't disagree. The problem was, I wasn't in charge. This was the first time in a while I'd fully unleashed Frank, and he was taking full advantage. He was having fun.

My body was covered in sweat as Frank continued to drain the life out of Foxglove.

She tried to choke out a word, but it was just a garbled sound.

Frank had too much control, and I was struggling to get it back.

Panic shot through a small part of my brain, but it wasn't enough to stop him. Nothing I did had any effect. He'd spent too long slumbering. Now that he was awake, he had no plans to back down anytime soon.

Foxglove slumped forward, her skin draining of color.

I roared and tightened my hold. Bloodlust consumed me. I wanted her dead.

"Tempest! Stop!" Axel's hands wrapped around my shoulders and yanked me backward.

I growled as I dropped Foxglove. My fingers sunk into his skin, and magic sparked across his flesh.

Axel ducked behind me, kicked my knees, and I hit the floor.

"Don't let Frank win," he said as he pinned me down. "You're better than he is. That's why you can always get back control. Goodness always wins against the dark. Fight him. Remember why you're doing this. Remember why you're here. You aren't a killer."

I snarled and bucked, shooting spells behind me to hit Axel, but he held on tight, no matter what I did.

His mouth pressed against my ear. "You're my friend. I'm on your side."

A breath shot out of me, and I slammed the barriers back on Frank, regaining a fragment of control. It was just enough to break through.

His anger echoed around my head and made me dizzy, but I was beating him. I could contain him.

"I'm good. You can let go." I staggered away from Axel and sucked in air.

His hand rested on my shoulder. "Everything okay?"

I glanced up and shoved my damp hair off my face. "It is now. Thanks."

He glanced at Foxglove. "I heard it all. Everything she said before I came into the room. I love my sister, but I can't support what she's done."

I nodded, grateful for his support. It was a hard decision to make, and I wouldn't forget he'd chosen me.

I stood, and the blood rushed to my head. As I staggered to the side, Frank took advantage of my weakness and regained control. I was hurled toward Foxglove before I could stop myself. My hands wrapped around her throat once again.

"Tempest!" Axel yelled.

Foxglove's eyes flickered open, and she smirked at me. "If I die, you'll never find out where your father is."

I jerked back, shocked at those words. My control of Frank snapped back into place.

"What do you mean? My dad's dead." My fingers loosened around her throat, and I stepped away, my insides shaking.

Axel was at my side, gripping my elbow. "Ignore her. She'll say anything to get what she wants. She's always been like that, ever since we were kids."

I shook my head. I had to know the truth. "What do you know about my dad?"

Foxglove remained on the ground, rubbing her neck. "Keep me alive and I might tell you everything."

Axel tugged me back a step. "Foxglove's playing with you. She must have heard about your father going missing, but that's all she knows."

"I'm so disappointed in you, brother," Foxglove said. "But you've made your choice. You pick the witches. Our father will be so embarrassed. He might even pay you a visit and make an example of you."

"Our father knows my situation." Axel glared at her.

"I don't care about your father," I said. "What do you know about mine? How do you know he's still alive?"

Foxglove chuckled. "Oh, he's alive. I always assumed he got bored with the family he'd been lumbered with and left Willow Tree Falls to find some adventure."

I snarled at her.

She launched off the ground, slamming into me and knocking Axel over. We rolled several times, magic sparking between us, but I couldn't get a clean shot to take her down. Could she know what happened to my dad? I couldn't believe he might still be alive. But what if he was? I had to know. And that meant Foxglove had to live.

We collided against the opposite wall, and she shoved me against it, her hot breath snaking across my face. "Say goodbye, Tempest Crypt." Her magic flared up between us.

Axel growled, pure rage on his face as he pulled his sister off me. Flames shot from his fingers and curled around her. "Leave my friend alone." He shoved Foxglove against the wall several times, until she was bound in his flames and motionless, a stricken look on her face as magic pinned her.

He placed his hand on her forehead. "You're ashamed of me! Trust me. It's the other way around. I can't believe you're my sister." He slammed his power into her, and she slumped to the floor with a gargled grunt.

Axel staggered back, the flames dying from his fingers and his breath shooting out.

I crawled across the floor, my head pounding and my stomach flipping over. "Are you okay?"

He nodded. "You?"

"I'll live." I slumped down. "Your sister?"

"Alive but trapped. I can't keep her like that for long. She's too strong." Axel knelt beside me and touched my hand gingerly. "I'm sorry. I didn't—"

"No! Don't do that. You helped me. That must have been hard to hear what she said."

He grimaced and looked away. "What do we do now?"

I looked at Foxglove, trapped in a prison of fire made by her own brother. "It's time to call in Angel Force."

Chapter 22

"Pass the croissants." Raine shoved an elbow into my ribs. "I'm not missing out on those."

I grinned as I passed her the basket of rapidly decreasing warm croissants.

It had been two days since Axel and I took down Foxglove. After she'd been restrained by Axel, the angels had arrived, taken in the chaos, heard his statement, and arrested Foxglove on the spot.

Mom touched my arm as she walked around the table. "How are you doing?"

"All's good here." I grabbed a breakfast scone and coated it liberally in strawberry jelly. Although, it wasn't, not really, and I had a feeling Mom sensed something troubled me. I hadn't stopped thinking about what Foxglove told me.

"Everyone's talking about what happened at Castle Falls," Granny Dottie said.

"I bet they are," I said. "It was all—"

"Mind if we join?" Rhett stood in the kitchen doorway with Axel.

I jumped from my seat and hurried over, kissing Rhett on the cheek. "Of course. You're always welcome. And you brought Axel."

Rhett shrugged. "He was lurking around outside. I took pity on him."

Axel grimaced, his usually confident demeanor absent as he rubbed the back of his neck. "I wasn't lurking. I wasn't sure you'd want to see me after everything that happened."

"Both of you join us. You're always welcome here." Mom pulled up two more chairs and shuffled people around, so it was an even tighter squeeze around the table.

Rhett settled in a seat next to me and squeezed my knee. "Everything sorted?"

I nodded. "Getting there."

"We were talking about all the fun Tempest's been having," Granny Dottie said. "Kidnapping, murder, and demons. All in our little village. Whoever said village life was boring has never been to Willow Tree Falls."

Axel winced and ducked his head. "I'm really sorry about Foxglove. If I'd known that's what she was planning, I'd have never let her stay. I didn't realize she'd gotten in with such a dark crowd."

"Tempest said something about a dark magic syndicate trying to take over the Magic Council," Auntie Queenie said. "Is that right?"

Axel shrugged and nodded a thanks to my mom as he accepted a plate full of maple syrup covered pancakes. "She didn't say much to me. I've only been able to talk to her for a couple of minutes since the angels took her. She mainly curses a lot, but it's all coming out. My sister is in it up to her neck with this syndicate."

"And Simone was going to reveal everything," I said. "She's the syndicate's weak link. She was a member but changed her mind when she fell in love."

"Love conquers all," Granny Dottie said.

"Not always," Aurora muttered.

I lifted my eyebrows at her. "Simone was going to testify against the syndicate, which would have ruined their plans, and they'd all go to prison. The Magic Council was supposed to protect Simone until she gave evidence and then relocate her with her fiancé, but John Smith was working for the syndicate. He informed Foxglove about Simone's whereabouts and put her at risk."

"My sister came to get rid of Simone and killed John when he got cold feet. She said he was a loose end." Axel stabbed a pancake.

"The same with Viggo," I said. "Foxglove didn't want anybody alive who could link her to these murders. She wanted a clean getaway."

Granny Dottie chuckled. "What an adventure. At least you got everything sorted. Good for you, Tempest."

"Axel helped." I glanced at him and nodded. I hadn't mentioned Foxglove's revelations about my dad to anyone else. Who could I talk to? Everyone thought he was dead. Or did they? Were they covering up something because they didn't want me to know the truth? Had he abandoned us? We were a little on the weird side, after all.

Aurora dropped a piece of strawberry onto her lap.

"What are you doing?" I asked.

She glanced at me and grinned. "Bonding with my new familiar."

I leaned across the table. Snuggled in her lap was Bandit munching on the strawberry.

"You're kidding me. You want Bandit as your familiar? You do know she's not even a true familiar?"

Bandit's head popped out from under the table, and she rested her chin on the edge. "I can be anything I choose. Since your attempts at undoing the spell on me have failed, I'm adjusting to my new situation. If that means I take on the esteemed role of being a white witch's familiar, then so be it. Aurora serves an excellent breakfast fruit platter, and her collection of scented bath bombs are out of this world. I smell like a summer flower meadow."

Aurora scooped up Bandit and kissed her head. "If it's okay with you, Tempest, I'd like her to move in with me."

"Of course," I said. "She's all yours."

"Although, I was thinking about a name change," Aurora said. "Bandit sounds fierce."

"Don't you want a warrior familiar?" I said. "What's more fearsome than Bandit?"

"How about Bambi?" She kissed Bandit's head.

She growled. "I'm not answering to Bambi."

"Or Bonny? That sounds sweet." More kisses hit Bandit's head.

"Is this some kind of unfunny joke?" Wiggles wriggled out from under the table and glared at Aurora. "You can't pick that mangy cat as a familiar."

Aurora laughed. "Why not?"

"He's jealous. I'm so cute, you'll forget all about the hound and his sulfur stink," Bandit said.

Aurora grinned and tickled Wiggles' chin. "I'll never forget you. I love you both equally." She shoved her chair back and pressed a kiss on Wiggles' head. "But you both need to call a truce. I can't have fights in my store every time you two meet."

"A truce?" Wiggles said. "With her?"

"Yes, with her," Aurora said. "Bambi is a part of our family now. That means we all need to get along. Shake paws."

Bandit hissed and retreated to Aurora's lap. "No name change and no truce, but I will tolerate him being in my presence."

"How gracious of you," I said.

Wiggles grunted, and smoke seeped out of his mouth. "Fine. I won't bite her unless she's really annoying."

"That's about as good as you're going to get," I said to Aurora.

"I'll take it," she said.

I sat with my family and friends for another few minutes as everyone talked over each other and stuffed themselves full of Mom's amazing breakfast.

I felt weird and out of place. I was keeping a secret, and it didn't feel good.

"I'll be back in a minute." I finished my scone and pushed my chair back. I needed some fresh air and quiet time to think about Foxglove's revelations. Had she been telling the truth? Was my dad out there somewhere, and he'd really just turned his back on us?

I slumped onto the porch and rested my chin on my hands.

"What's up with you?" Dazielle stopped by the garden gate.

"What's to say anything's the matter with me?" I pulled myself upright. "How are things with Foxglove?"

She grimaced. "They're moving slowly. She's being difficult, but we have all the information from Simone, plus your statement, along with Axel's and Trixie's. It all stacks up. We're using the information to track Foxglove's other contacts. This dark magic syndicate isn't going to cause problems anytime soon."

"That's good to know," I said. "What about Simone?"

"She's getting what she wants. A new identity and a move far away from here with her fiancé. And hopefully, she'll get some magic training. The whole station is covered in glitter."

I scratched my fingers through my hair, and my nails came away glitter encrusted. "You're not the only one who got glitter bombed by Simone. I'm glad it all worked out for her."

Dazielle shrugged. "I guess I should thank you."

"My interference helped again?"

"It sometimes does." Dazielle turned to walk away.

I stood and hurried to the gate. "Before you go, do you know anything about my dad?"

She turned, and surprise lit her face. "Nothing. I mean I know the basics. He disappeared one day and was never seen again."

I sighed. "Yeah, that's about all I know as well."

"Why do you ask?"

"It's nothing. I heard something, and it made me wonder about him. That's all."

"I can't help you with that." Dazielle's gaze lifted over my shoulder. "I'll be seeing you." She turned and walked away.

I looked around. Raine stood on the top step of the porch, her hands twisted together.

"Did you need an escape too?" I returned to the porch step and sat with her.

"I love our family, but they're so noisy they make my head ache," she said. "I'm only used to having to put up with Azura's noise when I'm at home. I don't know how you do it."

"Why do you think I got my own place over Cloven Hoof?" I smiled. "Although, I wouldn't have them any other way. They've always got my back, no matter how badly I mess up."

She nudged me gently. "Same goes for you. I would most likely be charged with murder by now if you hadn't kept prodding."

"I'm just glad I figured out what was going on," I said. The angels had dropped all charges against Raine. She was free to return to her covert operations role at the Magic Council.

"I owe you big time," Raine said. "I couldn't expose this operation. Everyone had worked so hard, but the dark magic syndicate was gaining power. I had to take the risk that the angels would work things out."

"That was a big risk, knowing what the angels are like."

"Yeah, I gathered that," she said. "I needn't have worried. You were here. You weren't letting go of this until you found the truth."

I shrugged. "You're family. I couldn't see you go to prison for something you didn't do."

"Girls, come back inside." Mom stood in the doorway. "I'm making more waffles."

Raine grinned. "Shall we face the noise for your mom's waffles?"

"Sure. They are epic." We stood and headed back into the house.

I paused and looked out along the lane. Things were good again. I was back with my family, the killer had been caught, and the village was safe. It would do for now.

But Raine was right. If there was truth to be found, I always hunted it down.

And if there was truth lurking out there that involved my dad and what happened to him, I needed to know what that was.

Wiggles bounded out and thumped into my legs. "You're missing all the food. And that smug cat is being annoyingly cute and forcing people to like her. She must be stopped."

I smiled at him. "I'm coming."

His head tilted. "What's up?"

I scooped him into my arms and kissed his ear. "Nothing now you're here."

He licked my cheek. "I'm the perfect fix for all worries. Let's go eat waffles. And then maybe pizza for lunch?"

I chuckled as I carried him back inside. Things weren't perfect, but they were good enough for now.

247

About Author

K.E. O'Connor (Karen) is a cozy mystery author living in the beautiful British countryside. She loves all things mystery, animals, and cake. When she's not writing about mysteries, murder, and treats, she volunteers at a local animal sanctuary, reads a ton of books, binge watches mystery series, and dreams about living somewhere warmer.

To stay in touch with the fun mysteries:

Newsletter:
www.subscribepage.com/cozymysteries

Website:
www.keoconnor.com/writing

Facebook:
www.facebook.com/keoconnorauthor

Also By

Luck of the Witch
Hell of a Witch
Revenge of the Witch
Curse of the Witch
Son of a Witch
Framing of the Witch
Trickery of the Witch
Wishes of the Witch
Harmony of the Witch
Remedy of the Witch
Gift of the Witch
Toil of the Witch
Jinxing of the Witch
Craving of the Witch
Union of the Witch
Chaos of the Witch
Sleighing of the Witch

If you enjoyed

Trickery of the Witch

turn the page to read an extract from the next Crypt
Witch Mystery

WISHES OF THE WITCH

Chapter 1

The steady fall of rain from the slate-gray sky matched my sour mood. I tapped my fingers on the top of a bar that had seen better days and tried to ignore my rumbling stomach. I was overdue dinner.

Five days out of Willow Tree Falls, and I missed everything about my wonderful, quirky village. I missed Mom's cooking and her interference in my love life, my sister's endless supply of brownies, the chilled vibe in my bar, and Wiggles. I missed him stealing my pillows, eating all the food, and making wisecracks.

I checked the time again and sighed. Isaac Dubrov was half an hour late.

As the minutes dragged by, my irritation grew. I didn't appreciate being stood up.

"Another drink?" The dull-eyed bartender nodded at my empty glass.

"Sure. Same again."

He refilled my glass with soda water and a wedge of lime and slid it toward me. "Your date's not shown up?"

"He'd better," I muttered.

"If he suggested meeting here, it's probably best he's a no show."

"This place was my suggestion." I'd noticed the bar when staking out the pizza parlor across the road.

The demon I was hunting had gone there every day, and this was the perfect location to meet Isaac and watch my prey.

"Better luck next time." The bartender shrugged and walked away.

No matter what town or city I came to when I left Willow Tree Falls, they all felt the same. They lacked that sparkle of magic that gave my home its unique feel.

I glanced around the bar at the handful of other patrons. How could humans live like this? There didn't seem to be any joy as they rushed around with panic in their eyes.

It was illegal to use magic around humans. Although, I got a hall pass when I was hunting a demon. However, if I decided to go on vacation and accidentally blasted a human with a memory wipe spell, I'd be hauled in front of the Magic Council to explain myself.

Palak, the demon I was chasing, was currently gorging himself on a family-sized deep pan meat feast pizza. I could just make out his hunched back and claws through the steamed window. To humans, he looked like an average guy, but I saw straight through his disguise.

That meal would keep him occupied for a while, which was perfect. He could eat, while I got the information I needed.

Isaac Dubrov was a trader who specialized in illegal magic spells. He had his ear to the underground magic grapevine and got to hear all the secrets, which was why we were meeting. I hoped he knew something about my missing dad.

A finger prodded my shoulder. "Need some company, hot stuff?"

I turned in my seat, my gaze running over the tall, stocky guy dressed in dark jeans and a navy-blue T-shirt that had seen better days. "My own company's more than enough to keep me entertained."

His brows lowered for a second. "So, you're a clever one? Like to joke?"

"I have a terrible sense of humor." I turned away, hoping he'd get the hint.

"I love funny girls." He settled on the stool next to me.

"Then go find yourself one."

He snorted a laugh. "Can I get you a drink?"

"I'm sure you can. The question is, should you?"

His forehead wrinkled. "Does that mean you want one or not?"

My patience was hanging by its last thread. This guy had better not push me or it would snap. "Find someone else to chat to. I'm waiting on someone."

"Husband or boyfriend?" An eyebrow arched. "Or a girlfriend? I don't mind. We're equal opportunities here."

"None of the above," I said.

"So, you're single?"

I lifted my gaze to the ceiling. Top marks for persistence, but he'd picked the wrong day to mess with me. "You need to look elsewhere."

"I'm just seeking out some fun." His hand slid down my arm. "You've been sitting on your own for ages. You must be lonely."

"I promise you, I'm not."

He was quiet for a second. "You must have an Irish heritage with that black hair and pale skin. It's sexy."

I shrugged. "I like potatoes and Guinness, if that's what you mean."

"Potatoes? I don't get it. You want me to take you out for some french fries?"

I sighed softly. I doubt this guy got much. "I'm sure the woman of your dreams is out there waiting for you. I'm not her. I don't want company. I'm waiting for someone. Take the hint."

He grinned. "I love it when a girl plays hard to get."

I closed my eyes. That was it. Patience officially snapped. I dropped a couple of barriers inside me, just enough to let Frank slide up my spine and warm my insides. When I flicked my eyes open, I locked gazes with the guy and bared my teeth.

He jerked back in his seat as if he'd seen something terrifying. He stared at me without speaking for several seconds. "Erm. Uh. I mean... I just remembered I need to be somewhere." He practically ran out of the bar.

"That's enough for now," I muttered to Frank as I pushed him back down.

Frank grumbled a few times but was content to slide away. Since we'd been away from Willow Tree Falls, I'd given him a whole day out. He'd had the freedom to roam wherever he liked. It meant I'd woken one morning with a banging headache and a hazy memory of breaking into a bakery and gorging on triple chocolate brownies, but he was sated. He'd had his freedom fix, and he was a happy little demon.

It was a shame the same couldn't be said for this miserable little witch.

I picked up my glass and took a sip. I was tempted to try something stronger, but every alcoholic drink I'd sampled on previous visits always left a sour taste. It was nothing like the single malt dwarfen whiskey I served in Cloven Hoof. And nothing held a torch to my speciality lemon drops.

I placed money on the bar and stood. I was done wasting time.

As I turned to the door, it swung open.

Isaac strolled in. He stood at an imposing six-foot five, dressed in a knee-length black frock coat and black jeans. He looked like a chunky pirate.

His gaze flitted across the few people in the bar before settling on me. He nodded and scrubbed a hand across his stubbled chin.

I lifted my own chin in response as my eyes slid to the enormous scarlet and blue parrot on his right shoulder. Yep, he was definitely going for scary pirate today.

Isaac inclined his head to a table at the back of the bar.

I grabbed more drinks and followed him to the gloomy corner. I settled on the seat opposite him and passed him a glass. "Did you forget we were supposed to be meeting?"

A cold smile slid across his face as he stroked a finger down the parrot's chest. "Timekeeping never was my speciality. When there's business to be done, it always takes precedence."

"This isn't business?"

The sides of his mouth turned down. "I've yet to decide. I'm not sure what you've got to offer me, Tempest Crypt."

"She's a pretty one," the parrot said.

"As are all the Crypt witches," Isaac said. "This is Crimson Squawker. I've had him twenty years. He's my right-hand man, well, bird. I'd trust him with my life."

"Nice to meet you, Crimson," I said.

"Mr. Squawker to you," Isaac grumbled.

I took note of the bird's sharp talons. "Mr. Squawker it is. So, I need information."

Isaac's gaze ran over me. "I was intrigued to come and find out more. You're looking for your father?"

I nodded. Ever since Foxglove Shadowsoul announced she knew my dad was still alive, I'd been unsettled. I had to know if it was true.

When I got offered a freelance job by Angel Force to go demon hunting, it gave me the perfect opportunity to do some digging and see if there was any truth to Foxglove's statement.

"He's been missing for ten years," I said.

"What happened?"

"He just disappeared," I said. "He went out one day and never came back."

"Problems at home?"

"Nothing he wasn't handling," I said.

"Marriage problems?"

"No. He loved my mom. She was heartbroken when he left."

"Sometimes, people can act heartbroken to cover up something."

I scowled at him. "Not my mom. They loved each other. Sure, they argued now and again, but they had a good relationship. His disappearance had nothing to do with her."

"What about you?"

"You think I did something bad to my dad?"

Isaac's tongue poked out from between his teeth. "You're the demon carrier. You've had that demon since you were a kid, haven't you?"

"You seem to know a lot about me." I rubbed my forehead. It seemed like everyone knew the story about me swallowing a demon to protect my sister.

"I like unusual things, and I collect strange information." He grinned slowly. "What's stranger than you?"

"Thanks for the compliment. My demon's under control. And he didn't get his demon claws into my dad. The last time I saw him, he was in Willow Tree Falls. Aurora was rushing us out the door to get to school, and I was dragging my heels."

"You didn't like school?" Isaac grinned.

"Not much. I can imagine you weren't a grade A student, either. Anyway, Dad walked us to the end of the lane, and we split up. It wasn't until we were all sitting around the dinner table that night, and he still wasn't home, that we began to worry. The last anyone saw of him, he was walking toward the magic barrier."

"He was leaving the village?"

I nodded. "That's right."

"Did he have anything with him?"

"Nothing. He left everything behind. All he had were the clothes on his back and whatever was in his wallet."

"What are his powers?"

"Is that important?"

"Power can enhance, but it can also extinguish," Isaac said. "What's to say your dad didn't turn rogue and simply decide to leave Willow Tree Falls in search of something more... enticing?"

Those words hit home, and I winced. They were similar to what Foxglove had said. "He was a good dad to my sister and me. His powers weren't excessive. He was a mid-level warlock."

"Nothing special about him?"

My throat tightened. "Everything."

Isaac smirked. "I mean, any unusual ability that might draw attention? Maybe he has a skill somebody wanted to acquire. It's not outside the realm of possibility he was taken and is being forced to work for somebody against his will."

"Is that what you've heard?" I leaned closer. "When I contacted you, you said you knew something about him."

Isaac sipped his drink and grimaced. "What's this?"

"Water. We both need clear heads."

He gestured to the barman. "Whiskey sour."

I rapped a finger on the back of his hand. "My dad? What do you know?"

He waggled his head. "Before I tell you anything else, let's organize our trade."

"What do you want?" I was too quick to speak, but I was getting desperate for information. Every lead I'd been following had quickly vanished.

Isaac's grin was sharp. "Be careful not to offer too much. I always collect."

"Spit it out." I glowered at him.

He lifted his palms. "I require a small thing. The final ingredient for the spell of vanquishing."

I grimaced and shook my head. "That's not happening. I'm not trading dark magic with you. A spell like that would mean trouble for both of us. Besides, who do you want to vanquish?"

He lifted a shoulder. "A witch of your renown must know that spell."

"Even if I did, you're not getting the information."

"I figured as much. Every list of ingredients is missing one vital element. I've been attempting to complete that spell for some time. It would be most useful."

"And you plan to vanquish..."

He shook his head and tapped the side of his nose. "That's my secret to keep. If not that, then how about you give me use of your demon for one day?"

I choked out a laugh. "You have no idea what you're asking. Frank isn't controlled by anybody when he gets loose."

"Ha! I heard that you called him Frank. He must enjoy that cute nickname."

"It riles him. I do it for my own amusement," I said. "But I can't lend him to you. He's unpredictable and dangerous."

"Which is exactly what I need for the task I have in mind."

"Frank's off the table," I said. "Ask for something else."

Isaac twisted his mouth to the side. "There's nothing you can offer me."

I wasn't letting him go without finding out what he knew. "Maybe you have someone causing trouble in your life. I hunt demons for a living. Any demon problems you need me to sort out?"

He chuckled. "A lot of my dealings involve demons. I can't tarnish my reputation by openly associating with a Crypt witch to get rid of my enemies."

"It's already a terrible reputation," Crimson Squawker said.

Isaac grinned. "You mean terrifying. But if you can't get me the spell I require, and I can't make use of your demon services..."

We were silent as the barman brought over his drink.

Isaac took a sip. "There is a trivial matter you can assist with. It's hardly worth mentioning."

I was walking into a trap, but I went there anyway. "What is it?"

"Tell me about Angel Force."

My head jerked back. I hadn't expected that. "Angel Force? Why do you want to know about them?"

"They're a thorn in my side," he said. "They illegally took my precious supplies."

"They took things that can be used as evidence against you?"

"What they have will never be traced back to me," he said, "but I need it returned."

"What is it?"

"A few trifling objects. Nothing to concern yourself with," he said. "The less you know, the better. All I need is the layout of the Angel Force building."

"So you can steal what they've taken?"

"You can't steal something if it already belongs to you," Isaac said. "I simply need to know the easiest way to get in, so I can locate my items, remove them quietly, and leave without anybody noticing. Nobody will get hurt."

My eyes narrowed. I didn't trust Isaac, but I was desperate to hear anything about my dad. I'd been following supposed leads and dead ends for three months. All I was getting was frustrated and convinced that what Foxglove had told me was a lie. But I couldn't let it go, not until I knew for certain.

"It's a simple enough request, Tempest," Isaac said. "I believe you have dealings with the angels from time to time. Isn't your current mission to deal with Palak authorized by them?"

I lifted my chin. "How do you know that?"

He raised his hands. "I'm a gatherer of useful information and a trader of knowledge. I know you work with them. You must have been inside their building. Simply tell me how to get in and out and leave the rest to me."

I debated this request as I sipped on my drink. "You're not going to hurt the angels?" I wasn't their biggest fan, but I also didn't like to think they'd be injured if I gave out this information.

"Hand on my blackened heart, those angels will know nothing about me being there. I'll be quiet, stealthy, and invisible. Unless they check their evidence store, they won't even know what's missing. It's a simple request. Give me the information, and I'll tell you what I know about your dad."

"I'll do it. But I don't want to learn you've destroyed the place and taken the angels out while you were there."

He chuckled. "I didn't know you cared about them."

"We rub along well enough most of the time. But if it gets back to them that I've helped you with this, that goodwill will disappear." And Dazielle would have another reason to dislike me.

Isaac nodded. "This is between us. Tell me everything you know."

I spent five minutes giving him the lowdown on the angels' building. He listened intently, Crimson Squawker also paying attention as I mapped out the layout and the easiest way to get in the building without being noticed.

Although I'd never been in the angels' evidence store, I had a pretty good idea where it was. It wouldn't be difficult to get in and grab what he needed.

"That's everything I know," I said. "Now, tell me about my dad." My pulse kicked as I waited for him to speak.

Isaac's finger idly stroked down Crimson Squawker's chest. "He's keeping off grid."

"You've seen him?" My heart thudded.

"I haven't seen him. But after you contacted me, I did some asking around. I learned more of his history, which corroborates everything you've said. He left your village and has been trying to make himself invisible ever since."

"I already know that," I said. "I want recent details. Has anyone seen him since he left Willow Tree Falls?"

He nodded. "Six months ago in the dark realm."

I swallowed, my throat tightening. "Doing what?" The dark realm was no place for any decent magic user. It was a place for outcasts, those wanted by the law, and magic users who had no respect for the natural order. Dad would never go there.

"Why does anybody go into the dark realm?" Isaac asked. "It's the perfect place to become a nobody. People don't care what you do in there. There are no laws. Even the angels keep away because they won't survive five minutes in that place."

"You must have heard something about why he went in there."

"No idea," Isaac said. "I could make suggestions, but I'd have no evidence to back them up. The last confirmed sighting of him was six months ago."

"Anything could have happened in that time." My hands landed flat on the table. "You must have more information."

"Nothing else."

My frustration and anger alerted Frank. He zoomed up my spine and tickled the back of my neck.

Isaac's nostrils expanded, and Crimson Squawker screeched. "Steady now, Tempest. I understand this is a difficult time for you, but your papa must be staying away for a good reason."

"He can't be doing this willingly," I said. "Has he been seen with anyone shady? Have you heard that anyone's been using him?"

"No, nothing like that. As far as I can tell, he's not in servitude to anyone. He just doesn't want to be around people anymore. He left you and the rest of your family to be on his own. Maybe he simply preferred it that way."

The idea lodged in my gut like a cold hard ball of something toxic. I'd wondered this myself. Dad had given up on us. He'd walked away from his family because he wanted something more. Our weirdness and strange ways had been too much for him.

"How do I know I can trust you?" I asked.

"If I lied to people who asked me to get accurate information, I wouldn't be alive and talking to you." Isaac's eyes blazed with indignation. "My word is my oath. I promise you, that's all the information I could find. My source is accurate."

"Who's your source? I have to meet them."

He waved a finger in the air. "No, that's not how we do things. I have my own connections within the community. I make use of them. You don't get to do that. Anything you need, you come through me. And if you want to validate what I'm saying, then go see your dad for yourself."

I raked a hand through my hair. I had no plans to go anywhere near the dark realm unless it was a last resort. People who went in often didn't come out. "That's all you've got to tell me?"

"For now," he said. "But you were generous with your information about the angels. I'll continue to seek reliable leads about your father. But he's been gone a long time and is doing an excellent job of keeping hidden. Have you thought that perhaps he's doing it for your benefit?"

"How is not having him around helping me?"

"He could have left because there was a problem he didn't want to inflict upon his family."

"Dad wouldn't do that," I said. "And he didn't have any problems big enough to make him walk away from us. We'd have helped, whatever it was. It can't be that."

Isaac's gaze lifted over my shoulder. "Well, that's all I can tell you. And if you want to catch that demon you're hunting, you need to get a wiggle on. He's about to make his move on a cute blonde. It would be a tragedy to see that pretty face spoiled because you got distracted on your mission."

I stood from my seat and stared through the grimy window of the bar. Sure enough, Palak was lurking in the shadow outside the door of the pizza parlor. The cute blonde in question was oblivious to his presence as she chatted on her phone and twirled a curl around one finger.

"One more thing. I..." I looked back at Isaac. His seat was empty. The only thing that remained was a single red feather from Crimson Squawker.

I stomped out of the bar, my demon target in sight and my anger blazing. This was just what I needed, a knockdown fight with a demon. I had to take my frustration out on something. What better than a misbehaving demon with cheese stuck to his chin?

And once I'd captured Palak, I needed to figure out my next move when it came to finding my dad.

What was he doing in the dark realm? And how was I getting him back?

Wishes of the Witch is available in e-book and paperback.